THE
GENERAL

And MONAVILLE, TEXAS

a novel

THE
GENERAL

And MONAVILLE, TEXAS

a novel

JOE G. BAX

EMERALD BOOK CO.
A Division of Greenleaf Book Group LLC

Published by Emerald Book Company
Austin, TX

Distributed by Emerald Book Company

For ordering information or special discounts for bulk purchases, please contact Emerald Book Company at PO Box 91869, Austin, TX 78709, 512.891.6100.

Design and composition by Greenleaf Book Group LLC
Cover design by Greenleaf Book Group LLC

Publisher's Cataloging-In-Publication Data
(Prepared by The Donohue Group, Inc.)

Bax, Joe G.
  The general and Monaville, Texas / Joe G. Bax. -- 1st ed.

  p. ; cm.

  ISBN: 978-1-934572-24-5

1. Ku Klux Klan (1915-)--Texas--Fiction. 2. Texas--History--1846-1950--Fiction. 3. Texas--Race relations--Fiction. I. Title.

PS3602.A9 G4 2009
810/.6   2009928587

Part of the Tree Neutral™ program, which offsets the number of trees consumed in the production and printing of this book by taking proactive steps, such as planting trees in direct proportion to the number of trees used: www.treeneutral.com

Printed in the United States of America on acid-free paper

09 10 11 12 13 14   10 9 8 7 6 5 4 3 2 1

First Edition

To Michele

CHAPTER I

Blue

CHINK. CHINK. PING. CHINK. CHINK. PING.

The sound was still rather faint, but it would grow louder as I approached Blue's barn. There was no need for a rooster in Monaville. Blue's clanging had been the morning's first sounds since my grandpa had moved Blue and his forge to town shortly after the War. My pace was a good bit slower today. My grandpa's large Percheron had seedy toe. Blue would have to reshoe the horse's hoof. The road from the Catalpa bottom to town had some rocky spots. There was no need to aggravate the hoof any more than necessary by rushing the horse.

Blue's barn sat behind the town between two of the largest cottonwood trees in the entire Brazos River bottom. Once I left the bottom, those treetops could be seen just to the left of the road. At the turnoff to the Oakridge Plantation, the treetops appeared on my right. So it went, back and forth, with almost every bend or turn, until I reached the edge of Monaville and started the climb toward Blue's barn.

Under the cottonwood trees at the back of the barn, I could now make out Blue's round frame. I knew to look under the cottonwood at the back of the barn. Chink, chink, ping meant that today Blue was carving a headstone. Someone had died, and enough time had passed since planting the beloved deceased to gather the money to pay for a stone. Blue didn't charge much. Despite the efforts of Monaville's resident capitalist, Colonel Reams Whitworth, Blue had only a rudimentary concept of money. Blue understood cotton, horseshoes, labor, or things to barter, but currency was beyond him, as it was beyond most of the recently freed South.

By now, the sounds were very clear and I could taste the Texas limestone powder thrown into the air by Blue and his chisel. The morning was still cool and the ground still wet with dew, but sweat dripped from Blue's forehead in torrents. It really did not matter what season it was or what task was at hand—Blue would be sweating.

Chiseling a name into rock required some strength, but not nearly the effort it took for Blue to build the wrought-iron fence for each grave in the Wilhite family cemetery. That effort was immense. Each picket was formed by huge swings of a heavy hammer that arched high over Blue's head before landing exactly where he intended them to land. If you wanted to see a man sweat, come by Blue's barn after a Wilhite had died.

I approached the barn from the rear. Shoeing the Percheron was going to take some time, and the tombstone looked like it would fill Blue's morning.

"Howdy, Blue."

"Howdy, John Ross. What's da problem with da big horse?"

"Seedy toe," I said. "Grandpa wants a bar shoe put on him while I doctor the infection."

"Just like da General. He ain't doin' no plowin', but he wants 'em ready anyhow."

Blue stayed firmly seated on his log bench. Everything about Blue was round. He was only about five-and-a-half feet tall, but he was all circles—a round, thick torso, not fat, but dense, on two barrel-shaped legs. You would expect a blacksmith to have large arms, but Blue's were huge round spheres hinged at the middle. If that weren't enough, his woolly hair, half white, had partially left him, leaving a perfectly round bald spot right in the middle of his head.

"John Ross, your friend Afton came by last night to check on da puppies. Da big one has his eyes open."

Normally, I didn't get upset at the mention of Afton. We had grown up together. But recently, people were placing an odd emphasis on the words "your friend." For reasons not totally understood by me, I felt my ears glow bright red whenever her name was mentioned.

"That's good. Blue, have you already hitched up Colonel Whitworth's buggy?"

"Yes, sir, but I would 'preciate it if you'd look at his nephew's horse. He said somethin' ain't right wif his mouf."

Any daylight coming in the front door was blocked when Colonel Reams Whitworth, all 300 pounds of him, glided in on two of the most pigeon-toed feet in the entire state of Texas. The Colonel didn't really enter a room; he inhaled it.

"Howdy, Blue."

"Mornin', sir."

"Did we make any money this weekend? Was the spoonin' and sparkin' surrey rented?"

"Rented every day, Colonel," said Blue.

"No one can say that Colonel Reams Whitworth isn't doing his part to repopulate the South. That courtin' carriage is just four years old and it's . . . well, parts of it are just about worn out. You know, Blue, the boys down at Nuncio's tavern call it the fornication wagon."

"Didn't know dat, sir."

"Howdy, John Ross. What critter are you doctoring today?"

"Grandpa's Percheron needs a different shoe and . . ." Before I could finish, the Colonel had relocated the conversation to another spot entirely.

"How is the General, John Ross?"

"He is well, sir."

"Let me guess. He left Catalpa before first light this morning dressed in the same gray coat he wore during the Rebellion or, shall we say, the late unpleasantries with our Northern brethren."

"I didn't see him, but I s'pect that's what he had on, sir."

"No doubt about it. His punctuality would be the envy of any railroad conductor. Your grandfather is without a doubt the dullest individual I have ever known. He is the only person I know who came home from the War, didn't even change clothes, and went right to work. The man is dull, I tell you. Despite his shortcomings, do give him my best.

"John Ross, isn't it about time you rented the courtin' carriage? I mean, for you and your friend Afton?"

There it was again—"your friend." Without question, my ears were afire. It seemed that all of Monaville had taken an inordinate interest in my so-called friend Afton. I thought the best strategy was to grin my way through a reply, but that didn't seem to be enough for Colonel Whitworth.

"Come on. I'll give you a special rate. It would give some of these dried-up old prunes something to talk about. And who knows, you might even have a good time." The Colonel was truly enjoying himself.

"What time do you have to be at school, John Ross?"

"Miss Hightower doesn't require me to be there until nine thirty."

"Nine thirty? Why so late?"

"It takes her that long to settle down the youngsters. Since I'm the oldest, she pretty much has me doing stuff on my own." I hoped that would satisfy him.

"Edwina Hightower. I have known that old scarecrow all my life. Used to go skinny-dipping down in the river."

"Miss Hightower, sir!" The thought and the imagery were more than my already-red ears could handle.

"Oh hell, John Ross. Back then, she wasn't nothing but a boy with a hole in the middle. It's good that you are sticking with your studies. Have you given any thought to going back East for college?"

"College, sir?"

"Now, boy, I know you have heard the word. You have a talent with and most certainly an interest in all these animals. It will be a long time before the South has anything or anyone who can teach you what there is to know. Give it some thought. Talk to your father, but I expect the problem will be the General."

"Haven't thought of it, sir, but I will." I did have some vague notion about college. Grown-ups had mentioned it before, but I hadn't paid any particular attention. As far as anything to do with the eastern part of the country, particularly the Northeast, I had my doubts. The Yankees may have won the War, but they did not win Grandpa's respect, not one bit.

Each morning the Colonel would ride out to his birthplace, the Oakridge Plantation, to visit "his people," although he now called them "his customers." Blue positioned the Colonel's buggy so that he could climb into it. The Colonel grabbed the front edge of his buggy while his team took a wide stance in order to support the tug that his girth would require as he struggled to gain access to the spring-supported seat. The entire buggy frame tilted dangerously in the direction of the Colonel.

"Colonel, I must have a word with you right now." Ocy McCoy appeared more than a little agitated. Frankly, Ocy had seemed agitated since Juneteenth, the day the slaves in Texas had been told they were free. Actually, they had been free for some time, but no one had bothered to tell them. Ocy, like so many sharecroppers, was attracted to the river bottom for the same reasons it drew the early settlers. Cotton had been king. They had hoped it would be their path to prosperity.

Colonel Whitworth eased his large mass back down to the ground, much to the relief of the horses. He gradually turned to face Ocy. Expressionless, but with eyes intently focused on the dirty, muddy face of McCoy, the Colonel said, "You hear that, Blue, this fellow must have a word with me."

Blue busied himself with the headstone, hoping that the Colonel didn't require his participation in any conversation with Ocy McCoy.

"And what brought you out beyond the tree line this morning, Mr. McCoy?"

McCoy was a wiry, bony sort, with one lazy eye, who was dwarfed by the Colonel. Nonetheless, he was so mad that he spoke in clipped sentences.

"I was down at your store. They wouldn't sell me any provisions, no seed, no nothin'."

"That's correct. They are acting on my instructions."

"But Colonel, how is a man supposed to survive if . . ."

"Mr. McCoy, you haven't paid me a dime on your account in four years. You have never bothered to even broach the subject with me. You come into my store, finger everything in the entire place, gather whatever you want, and expect my clerks to figure out just exactly what you took. It seems to me that your idea of a mercantile relationship differs from mine by no small amount."

"Mercantile?"

"Business relationship. That is what we supposedly have, a business relationship. I sell goods, you pay for what you buy, or in this case, take."

"We croppers have good and bad years, Colonel."

"I am keenly aware of that, except that you are more consistent than most. Your years are consistently bad. Even when everyone else is awash in cotton, your crop is not only thin, it is downright poor. And it's your own damn fault."

"Colonel, how would you know?"

"My father established the Oakridge Plantation many years ago. I was born and raised on it and I think I have some idea of what it takes to grow a bale of cotton. The Good Lord decides how much rain we will get and whether he will let that crop make. But if you don't pay attention to your business, and you don't, your crop is never going to make."

"What do you mean? I pay . . ."

"No, sir, you don't." The Colonel didn't let him finish. "You and that white-robed group of Klansmen spend way too much time riding around in your white sheets trying to scare hardworking folks off their land so that you can grab it. As long as all of us unreconstructed Confederates are disenfranchised, you and our wonderful district attorney, T. Roliff Harrington III, think you are the law unto yourselves. The worm will turn one of these days, McCoy. In the meantime, you Kluxers had better stay clear of Oakridge and the folks out there."

"I can't believe any white man would give land away to a bunch of darkies and not even sell me what I need to make a living."

"We are finally getting to the crux of the issue, aren't we?"

"Those coons can't make it no way. They are ignorant, just ignorant."

"Fortunately, McCoy, those people at Oakridge have grown cotton on the same land for years, decades even. It would seem to me that giving a man the 50 acres that he plowed for years isn't much of a gift. Plus, I now have sixty-five very loyal customers. More important, they know the land and what it takes to raise a crop. Not that it's any of your business, but their accounts are paid and yours isn't. Now, who is the ignorant one?"

Ocy McCoy was visibly shaken and annoyed at the same time. Every ounce of muscle in his skinny body ached to inflict some hurt, preferably mortal, on the Colonel. McCoy didn't have the vocabulary to respond and didn't have the good sense to keep quiet.

"What you did was wrong and you'll pay for it."

"What are we talking about, McCoy? My giving land to my people or my refusal to sell you anything?"

"I'll get what I need somehow, but you'll pay for favoring those darkies."

"Let me ease your very simple little mind. When I decided to deed some of my land to help my people get a start, you and your fellow Kluxers were never in the running. So there was no favoritism. Since you don't seem to get it, let me be very clear. I didn't give the land away so that a collection of parasites could come and steal it. You and your fellow night riders are not to molest anyone at Oakridge. Please give my regards to your Mr. Harrington."

With a good deal more grace and ease than his first attempt, the Colonel pulled himself into the buggy, gathered the reins, and with a single snap, left Ocy McCoy pondering his last words.

Ocy McCoy hesitated for a moment, looked at Blue, then me, and then where the Colonel's buggy had been, then he headed off for parts unknown. I inhaled for what felt like the first time since the Colonel had said good morning.

"Blue, what is a Kluxer?"

"Idn't it time for school, John Ross?"

It was the response I expected. My grandpa says that I don't seem to have a shortage of questions. However, it seems that my questions tend to fall into a couple of groups. Most of the time, I get an answer, one that is generally correct. Sometimes, I get an answer that isn't correct. Other times, my questions get avoided or flatly ignored. Judging from Blue's increased attentiveness to the headstone, this was one that was going to get ignored or avoided.

"Aw, Blue, I know you know, now what's a Kluxer?"

"My goodness, son, dis why I hated to leave Catalpa and move to town. A black man can get in whole lots of trouble in town. Talkin' about Kluxers is one of da worst ways."

"Blue, ain't nobody here but you, me, and some animals, who ain't talking."

"You ever watch your chickens roost at night?"

"Sure."

"You see dey roost in da same spot every night next to da same chicken. If Momma Mae cooks one of dose chickens, then there's a fuss over who is going to roost where da chicken you ate used to roost."

"I've lived with chickens all my life. How does this explain Kluxers?"

"Before da War, der was a peckin' order. Everybody knew where dey fit. Slave times may haf been hard times, but everybody knew what to do and who to see about dis and dat and what was 'spected. White folks, all white folks, were on da top perch and all slaves were on da bottom perch.

"Now, dere ain't no slaves. I'm pretty sure most of da white folks are still on da top perch, but Mr. McCoy may not be so sure.

"When Colonel Whitworth gave his people land, it upset da whole chicken coop. Mr. McCoy don't own no land. He's a cropper. Your grandpa's people who stayed at Catalpa are croppers, but farming land a good bit better dan what Mr. McCoy's farming. Colonel Whitworth's people aren't croppers at all. Dey own land since da Colonel gave it to 'em. Some, like Big Charlie, are doin' pretty good."

"Grandpa sold a mule to Big Charlie just last week."

"Oh, Lord. See, dat has got to upset Mr. McCoy. He's pure cropper. He doesn't own land, plows, or mules."

"So I guess Mr. McCoy is mad at Colonel Whitworth."

"He's mad at da Colonel. He's mad dat da peckin' order has been upset. I s'pect he's mad dat his land's not very good. He's mad at things I can't even guess. But most of all, he don't want freed folks gettin' ahead of him. From what da Colonel just said, they already ahead."

"And the Kluxers?"

"John Ross, you best keep this to yourself. Mr. McCoy and others puts on sheets and robes and try to frighten' da black folks."

"What do they do?"

"So far, mischief mostly, but things gettin' a little serious at Oakridge. Fires, cattle kilt, and a few darkies beat up, but it seems to be gettin' worst."

"Do you know who the others with McCoy are?"

"I ain't seen no sheet, robe, or tarp big enough to hide a horse." Blue gave me one of his rare, but largely toothless, smiles.

"Blue, I haven't seen any of them try anything at Catalpa."

"I truly believes dat no one in dis county wants to get on the bad side of da General. Plus, he and your pa are always 'round. Da Colonel lives in town now so Oakridge is run by his people and Big Charlie.

"Plus da Oakridge people vote."

"What does voting have to do with it?"

"You have to figure dat out. All I know is most of da white men can't vote, at least not dose dat fought along wif da General. And dey don't like who everyone else votes for. The black folks used to vote—was all excited 'bout it when dey got to vote. Now it's mostly da Oakridge folk dat vote."

"Do you vote, Blue?"

"No."

"Why not?"

"You need a last name. After 'mancipation, all dese crazy darkies started takin' all kinds of names. No rhyme to it. Some took names dey liked or had heard of. Some named themselves after presidents . . . like dey ever knew a president. Ders enough named after President Lincoln to start a small town. My name is Blue. It has always been Blue and it works just fine. Plus, I'm doin' the best I can to figure out what I'm s'posed to do during freed times. Ain't been no rules set, so I'll just stay Blue."

I figured I had pried more out of Blue than he liked. Sometimes Blue's responses didn't complete the entire puzzle, but what Blue said was always Gospel, or at least the Gospel according to Blue.

CHAPTER 2

Catalpa

CATALPA PLANTATION RAN ALONG the meanderings of the Brazos River. The land gently rolled back from the east bank, which at times was mostly floodplain. At other points, it was all bluff. The bottomland contained the rich alluvial soil that had supported Catalpa Plantation's cotton operations from antebellum times through the War years. Since returning, the General had leased most of the cotton fields to sharecroppers—some were former Catalpa slaves; others were just croppers from wherever. The uplands now supported the General's cattle operations. He had seen enough violence and harm caused by the so-called unifying Southern cotton culture. His croppers were free to grow cotton, but the General wasn't going to—not any longer. This removed and separated him from the community, the routine of planting and harvesting the crop, and more important, the bonds and camaraderie of the men at the cotton gin. All of which suited the General just fine.

The Wilhites had settled all along the river. Catalpa had been the jumping-off place for most. They arrived in Texas in a steady stream, and once on their feet, they sought their own land. Catalpa was the oldest of the Wilhite plantations.

The home had started as a dogtrot made of logs. A second story was soon added. With so many traveling relatives, labor—black and white—was readily available. What had originally been the central breezeway was now the central hallway, with a finished staircase leading to the second floor. Most people would assume it was a typical Louisiana plantation home. However, the Wilhites had made a number of changes that gave it a Texas flair—columns were not round, but square, and although the windows went to the floor just like they did in Louisiana, the headers were flat topped, not arched.

The home sat among a grove of catalpa trees mixed with some cedar elms. If the catalpa trees gave the site its name, the cedar elms gave it its luster. Each tree was covered with millions of deep green leaves the size and shape of a single fingerprint.

Immediately behind the main house was the kitchen, the only building built of stone. A huge table, not for eating, but for the preparation of the meal, ran down its large cooking area. Momma Mae's personal quarters were toward the back. No one knew her age and no one dared to ask. She had been cooking at Catalpa since slave times, and so she continued.

The slave quarters had been just a hundred feet east of the house, down a lane that sloped away from the kitchen. Only a couple of the slave cabins remained. A good many had been dismantled and hauled to Monaville to be resurrected in the form of Blue's Livery Stable, Barn, Coffin, and Headstone Operation. Some folks could pick out the boards that had come from their cabins, or at least they said they could.

Any of Catalpa's now freed people who wanted to try their hand at sharecropping were permitted to move their cabins to the area of the cotton fields that they wanted to plant. This wasn't all that difficult. Skids were built, placed under the cabin, and hitched to the draft horses and mules. In a single day, cabins left the area of the big house and pioneered their way to the bottomland. Folks who had been neighbors in the quarters placed their cabins next to those same folks in the bottomland. By the end of the third day, chimneys were erected and the menfolk were prepared to start working the fields—the same ones they had worked for years. But this time, they had more to gain and more to lose.

Other buildings were opposite the remaining slave cabins. The horse barn had been expanded since the War. Not that the plantation needed more horses; the General just liked horses. The gardens, chicken coop, and working sheds were all within sight of the main house, which is exactly the way the General wanted them.

When my father and mother had married, the General had the home clad in finished boards and painted white. He felt some improvement was necessary because Catalpa would now be the home of a lady. A lady, certainly a proper Southern lady, needed a suitable home. The exterior and the downstairs interior were finished just before the War began.

The second floor still showed the hand-hewed logs. The General and I occupied the upstairs. My parents, Luther and Devon, and the twins occupied the first-floor rooms.

Each evening, when the General ascended the stairs, he headed back in his mind to that moment that had been interrupted by the War. At the top of the first flight of stairs, he transitioned from a Southern gentleman in a fine home to just another Texan trying to improve his lot in life. He would sit quietly for a moment, no doubt recollecting a thousand memories. He would slowly roll up his right pant leg to just below the knee. The buckles and leather straps would be sweat stained, but with a tug, he could remove the wooden peg that replaced what had been his leg. A Minnie ball had shattered his lower leg beyond any use. Blue had done a remarkable job. As soon as the leg had been removed, Blue began taking measurements. Bois d'arc wood was the material he chose because he knew it was the hardest. He fashioned a bowl at the top of the peg and lined it with the softest goose down he could find. The entire contraption fit like it was supposed to on the first try. Blue affixed straps to the fender of the General's saddle so that he could tie the wooden leg down. This wasn't needed very often. A small hole was drilled into the stirrup the size of the peg. With the stirrup modified, the peg fit right into it and the General was as mobile as ever.

Before first light, the General would strap on his leg and head downstairs. Moving from the unfinished second floor to the completed first floor only exaggerated his sense of impatience. He must find a way to make up for the loss of the War years. To the General, the loss was staggering and not just in time, money, influence, and power. It was the frustrating loss associated with a bad decision that had proven so costly.

The bois d'arc peg landed on every other step, striking a slow cadence. Today was Saturday, which did nothing to modify the General's routine. However, it did mean that I could accompany him all day, which I tried to do whenever possible.

While Momma Mae and the General exchanged "Good mornings," I headed to the barn to saddle the horses. I saddled the red-blooded bay for my grandpa. The bay took more time because he was such a big horse, and having inherited my mother's stature, I was below the horse's withers. My horse, being smaller, posed no problem. Grandpa took his breakfast in the house or on the porch if weather permitted. I preferred to eat with Momma Mae in the kitchen. To me, the food tasted better there. Plus, it was a safe haven from my sisters, and I needed a safe haven from my sisters—particularly redheaded twin sisters.

Momma Mae hummed constantly. She would stop and talk if you wanted her to, but if conversation wasn't on your mind, she just hummed. This was a welcome respite from my identical sisters, who started and completed each other's sentences, much to the frustration of the entire family. By themselves, they were almost a unit and they had a great deal of curiosity about everything I did: "What are you doing? Where are you going? Why did you do that?" Momma Mae's kitchen was just the sanctuary I needed.

The smells were absolutely wonderful. The morning aroma was always a mixture of fresh-baked breads, frying eggs, and sizzling ham or bacon. This didn't change even during the War. Those staples were always available. Apparently, the hens never thought to stop laying, and there were certainly enough feral hogs in our area to keep a family fat for years.

Later, if you concentrated, you could catch the scent of the evening meal. Certain things just go together. One whiff of an ingredient would tip you off to Momma Mae's evening fare. All of her meals were highly seasoned. If you didn't like food with a spicy little kick to it, this wouldn't be the place for you.

Legend has it that the General returned from the War and went right to work. He didn't even change his clothes. That part of the tale is correct. However, I assure you Momma Mae fed them all before they did anything. I vividly remember my grandpa, my father, Blue, Big Charlie, Colonel Whitworth, and the other men returning.

When my grandpa finished breakfast, he would head to the barn. As he passed the kitchen, he would call, "John Ross." Nothing more—just John Ross. Inside the kitchen, Momma Mae would interrupt her humming to tell me he had called for me. This apparently was a habit she developed when I was younger and a good deal less prompt.

"Good morning, Grandpa."

"Horses saddled, John Ross?"

"Yes, sir."

"Good. We have ground to cover."

This I already knew. He was so precise, so predictable; I bet the hooves of his horse hit the same hoofprints made the day before and the day before that.

It was barely first light as he stepped up and swung himself onto his horse. No need to strap his wooden leg down. The ride would be long, but easy. His bay was as surefooted as any horse I had ever seen. He was getting some age on him, but he was still a majestic saddlebred gelding. I would ride on Grandpa's right, a good deal closer to the ground. My Appy didn't have the height of the bay. We passed the house. My parents and the twins were still eating. That was good. I had the jump on them. Soon the twins would be old enough to figure out Grandpa's routine. For now, it was still a mystery to them. I hoped to keep it that way as long as possible.

We headed down the lane toward the Monaville road at a trot. Just as we were about to turn, Grandpa's horse shied in my direction, almost slamming into me.

"Whoa, horse." Grandpa brought him to a stop and turned to the left to see what had caused the reaction.

Gustav Weiberg stepped out from behind a yaupon tree and moved toward the center of the road.

"General, I'm very sorry to have startled you, sir, but I knew you'd be passing this way and I must speak with you." The General's routine was his downfall; apparently the whole town knew about it.

"Mr. Weiberg, think nothing of it. This horse is getting along in years and has a touch of moon blindness, as probably do I."

"General, I must ask a very great favor of you. I have no right to request it. You hardly know us, this being our first year on your place."

"Mr. Weiberg, if I can do it, I will; if I can't, then I can't."

"Our Sarah died last night. She's the second child we've lost. The last one, a boy, we buried in Alabama. My wife mourned so. She was almost beside herself when we had to leave him. She just can't get over that one of her children is lying in an unmarked grave that she will not likely see again."

My grandpa's eyes focused totally on Mr. Weiberg. He said nothing, but let him tell his story.

"We're poor croppers, but we work hard. I have hopes for the crop we've planted. The soil is certainly better than some of the other places we've lived. But even so, only the good Lord knows if we'll be able to make it here. My wife just can't think of leaving little Sarah in some unmarked grave. Not again, no, sir. She asked me to see if Sarah could be buried in your cemetery. I know she isn't a member of your family. I don't even know if this is proper or done. But I promised her I'd ask you."

Weiberg was a man of average height, but sharecropper skinny. As I watched the two men talk, the contrast was telling. Grandpa, astride the large bay, with the rigid bearing you would expect of a General, dwarfed Gustav Weiberg standing barefooted and poor.

"How long have you been waiting here for me?"

"I don't really know, sir. Sarah passed about dusk yesterday . . . it took me forever to quiet her mum . . . well, and the other kids. I promised them I'd ask you, and I started out to make sure I could catch you."

"You must be very hungry."

"I really don't even know, sir."

"If you don't mind me asking, Mr. Weiberg, how did Sarah die?"

"Same as our boy. She developed lesions, then diarrhea, just became lifeless, and in the end, there were fits."

"What are you eating?"

"Sir?"

"What do you have to feed your family?"

"Cornmeal, some flour, and whatever fish or game I can catch."

"I have absolutely no objection to having Sarah buried in our cemetery. It would be my honor."

"Sir, I'll be happy to dig the grave . . ."

"Now, that is not possible, sir. For reasons I have never fully understood, the Wilhite Cemetery is Blue's special project since the death of his sister, Elisabeth. I am sure you know Blue. He digs the graves. He decides where folks are to be buried. He sets the head-stones and anything else that he deems proper. I am sure there is some rhyme or reason to where he puts folks and why he does these things. At any rate, Blue will be happy to take care of Sarah.

"But first, John Ross will take you back to our home. You two make some noise when you approach Momma Mae's kitchen. I assure you she is someone you don't want to surprise. John Ross, while Mr. Weiberg has breakfast, go out to the garden and pick him some greens . . . anything green—no corn.

"Now, Mr. Weiberg, are any of your other children looking poor or in ill health?"

"None of them look too good, sir."

"I want you to come back next week and get some more greens. We don't have that many folks to feed anymore, but we still put in the same size garden. Force of habit, I expect.

"John Ross, you and Mr. Weiberg take the greens to their place and let Mrs. Weiberg fix them as she desires, but get your children to eat them as soon as possible.

"Mr. Weiberg, you have your wife write out what she wants on Sarah's headstone. You and John Ross will take that to Blue."

"Blue can read, sir?" This was not an unusual question given Blue's previous status as a Catalpa slave.

"Blue reads as well as I do. We both learned how about the same time. I suspect he can probably read better than I can now. Blue will make the coffin. The headstone will come later, but I assure you that it will come. All the graves, well, almost all of them, have headstones. Blue will see to it."

"Sir, how will I pay you? I must pay you, we're . . ."

"Mr. Weiberg, I have done nothing. That land is a cemetery. It has no other purpose. We shall all end up in one sooner or later. You have provided me with an opportunity to give some comfort to your family. I am the one in your debt, sir. I have a keen appreciation for the grief of a parent. Many parents in this country have suffered the loss of a child."

"Thank you, sir."

"Do you know Big Charlie of the Oakridge Plantation?"

"I've heard of him, but I really haven't met many folks around here."

"I don't want to tell you your business, but a garden is as important to you as that cotton crop. Most sharecroppers plant nothing but cotton from can see to can't. Your children need their greens. Visit with Big Charlie. He can grow anything anywhere. He can tell you what you ought to plant to eat. He is someone you need to know. In the meantime, come by the plantation every so often and get some greens.

"John Ross, go with Mr. Weiberg to Momma Mae, then to his family, and then to Blue."

"Yes, sir."

I knew better than to offer Mr. Weiberg my horse. As poor as he looked and was, he still was a working man and had his pride. He walked along beside me as we approached Momma Mae's kitchen.

I shouted for Momma Mae.

"John Ross, why is you back? Is der somethin' wrong? Is your grandpa okay?"

"Momma Mae, this is Mr. Weiberg. His daughter passed away yesterday. Grandpa said to give him breakfast, and I'm supposed to pick some greens."

"Good Lord. Mr. Weiberg, please come in and sit down. We gots plenty and it will be ready shortly."

I started gathering a basket full of greens. I had no idea how many younguns Mr. Weiberg actually had, but Grandpa seemed to feel they needed greens, so greens they would get.

As I turned to enter the kitchen, I heard the irritating sounds of the twins, all giggles and stumbles. No doubt they must have been intertwined before birth because they could not take more than four steps without bumping into each other or something else. This was not the time for them to meet Mr. Weiberg. I arrived in the kitchen too late. There they were, four hands on the table, two noses and four eyes just above its surface, peering right at Mr. Weiberg.

"Y'all get on out of here now, ya hear?"

Nothing but giggles.

"John Ross, what is the problem?" My mother always came to the defense of the redheaded hellions.

"Momma, can't you make them leave?"

"They have every right to be here. Oh, I *am* sorry, sir; I didn't see you. I'm Devon Wilhite."

Gustav Weiberg by now was pretty much speechless, standing before more folks than he had seen in months. To add to the gathering, my father also arrived.

"Why didn't you tell us we had company?"

Now I was speechless. I was following the instructions of my grandpa to the letter. Things were going well until the twins . . .

"Sir, this is . . ."

"Yes, John Ross. I know Mr. Weiberg."

"Pa, Grandpa and I met him on the road. He lost his daughter yesterday. Grandpa wants me to take some greens to his family and him to Blue for a tombstone."

"Oh, no." My mother was now quite shaken, and from my vantage point, appeared ready to take over the conversation.

"Mr. Weiberg, we are so sorry. How did she die?"

"Same as our boy back in Alabama—fever, diarrhea, fits. My wife begged me to ask the General if she could be buried in your cemetery. She still can't stand . . ."

"Do you have anything to bury her in? I mean, clothes."

"We all only have what we have on."

"I'll find something for the child. How old was she, Mr. Weiberg?"

"She was twelve, but very small for her age."

"John Ross, please prepare the buggy. I will take the greens and some clothes to Mrs. Weiberg. Mr. Weiberg can ride with me."

"Momma, I was supposed to take him to Blue. That's what Grandpa told me to do."

"I understand. I'm sure I can find their place. I'll deliver the greens, and I am certain I can find something suitable to bury your daughter in, Mr. Weiberg."

Fortunately, my pa had the good sense to use that short pause to suggest that my mother go look for the dress and take the twins with her. He turned to Mr. Weiberg.

"We all share your loss, Mr. Weiberg, and will do whatever we can to assist you. I suspect that your wife could use another woman to talk to about such things. Devon is a very good listener. John Ross will take you to Blue. In the meantime, I'll leave you to your breakfast. I'm sure you are quite hungry. Good day, sir."

At last, the commotion was over. I saddled a horse for Mr. Weiberg and hitched a team to the buggy for my mother. She left Catalpa armed with plenty of produce before Mr. Weiberg finished his breakfast.

The trip into Monaville was one of those awkward life experiences that I guess we all have to endure so that we can say we have reached adulthood. I had no idea what to say to Mr. Weiberg or if I should say anything. I chose to keep as quiet as possible. Since he hadn't seemed to know Big Charlie, I called his attention to the turnoff to Oakridge and told him where he could find Big Charlie. Grandpa seemed to think that was important.

I was grateful when Blue's barn came into view. Now I would have someone to share the heavy burden of conversation. Mr. Weiberg spoke before I could organize my thoughts.

"I'm Gustav Weiberg, a cropper out on the Catalpa Plantation. Our daughter Sarah died last night. General Wilhite has given us permission to bury Sarah in the Wilhite family cemetery. The General said I should see you about the details. I know this is unusual to have someone outside the family buried there. I guess Sarah will be the first?"

Blue stood directly in front of his anvil, taking in everything this stranger was saying. Weiberg's question called for some response and Blue gave an odd one.

Blue paused for some time. Then, looking away from Mr. Weiberg, he said, "I s'pose dat is mostly true."

Weiberg explained the death of his son and how his wife couldn't bear the thought of an unmarked grave for Sarah.

"Sir, how big was your daughter?"

"How big?"

"Yes, sir. I have some boxes already made. I keeps a small supply 'cause da Good Lord never gives me no notice when he's gonna call someone home."

Mr. Weiberg and Blue found a coffin they thought would work.

"Sir, where you wanna have da service?"

"I really don't know. We aren't churchgoing folks, being new here. We don't know anyone or . . ."

"Da rabbi just left and is headed downriver, da preacher is always here, and da priest will be here 'bout a week."

"I'm sure the preacher will do . . . can you tell me how to find him?"

"I s'pect he's at da church. It's da new Baptist Church, just west of town."

Mr. Weiberg turned and began to walk in the direction Blue had indicated. He was thin as a rail head on, but from the rear, he was downright bony. His homespun shirt had no more fullness to it than if it had been hung on a skeleton. What passed for trousers were tied to his waist with a cotton rope, yet he did not appear ashamed or overly sensitive about his meager appearance. Poverty had obviously been with him for quite some time. He had to provide a decent burial for his daughter. Nothing else mattered.

Blue seemed to be lost within himself. He had been out of sorts since the talk about the cemetery. I broke the silence that had settled over him and brought him back to the present.

"Blue, do you have a place in mind for her?"

"Huh? Uh, I s'pect I can find one. Dat's what da General wants."

"Sad, isn't it?"

"Yes, I builds dese boxes. They're all the same 'ceptin for size. But everyone's passing is different. You jus don't knows. Da older I gets, da more da death of young folks touches me . . . just touches me. Old folks, well, dey had their time, but younguns jus didn't even get a good start. Da War took so many away. If it had lasted much longer, I don't think I could've taken it. There wasn't enough of some of dose boys left to even bury. It makes you think too hard. Sometimes it isn't good to think too hard."

*   *   *

Devon Wilhite knew better than to take the twins. Knowing that Mrs. Weiberg had just lost a daughter, she realized that the sight of the young girls might bring back memories that were too fresh.

Devon Wilhite had never visited the sharecropper part of Catalpa. Monaville ladies of her stature just didn't ride the fields of the Brazos River bottom. However, it could be easily seen from the high road to Monaville. Finding the Weiberg home would be easy enough. The sight of her and the buggy would be a curiosity, and she knew most of the croppers, or at least those from Catalpa. After a couple of inquiries, she was directed to a tent under the only tree of any size in the middle of the cotton field.

The tent was old, worn, and patched, but still bore the faded "CSA" of the Confederacy. Things were quiet and still when she pulled her buggy up to the tent where the Weiberg family lived. Like all croppers, every square inch of land had cotton growing on it. There was barely enough space to turn around in, much less engage in anything other than growing cotton. From the tent stepped a small, worn woman, probably Devon's age, but looking a great deal older. Immediately behind her was a waif of a girl. Both were dirty and thin, and looked drained of any emotion.

"Mrs. Weiberg, I'm Devon Wilhite. Your husband told us of your great loss. I thought I might let you look through some of these dresses to see if one would work for your Sarah."

"You mean Sarah can have a burial in your cemetery?"

"I'm sorry, yes. I forgot that Mr. Weiberg went directly to town to make the arrangements."

Mrs. Weiberg collapsed, sobbing. A teenage boy ran to help her up and took her into the tent.

"I'm sorry, ma'am, please come in. My mother hasn't been well since Sarah passed."

Mrs. Wilhite gathered the dresses and started to pick up the basket of greens and other vegetables, but the young man came back out to help her.

Inside, the tent was clean and surprisingly well arranged. Mats of moss and grass were located around the perimeter. In the far corner lay Sarah, who even in death was a pretty child, with refined features. Mrs. Wilhite could easily identify with Mrs. Weiberg's loss.

"I am so grateful. I couldn't bear to leave another child in an unmarked grave," said Mrs. Weiberg, wiping her eyes with a corner of her sleeve.

"Yes, Mr. Weiberg told us. This won't be the case with Sarah. Blue shall dig the grave, provide the coffin, and carve the stone."

"Stone?"

"Yes, ma'am. I don't know what arrangements have been made between the General and your husband, but I feel fairly confident Blue will set a stone.

"Mrs. Weiberg, these dresses . . . well, I will leave them with you. Our girls have outgrown them. I see you have a younger daughter and I am sure she might enjoy them."

"But Mr. Weiberg don't accept no charity."

"Mr. Weiberg is a man. It is unlikely that he would even notice." The comment almost provoked a smile from Mrs. Weiberg.

"The General wanted me to make sure your family got these vegetables and greens. He suspects that whatever made Sarah sick had something to do with her diet. We have a large garden, frankly an exceptionally large garden. When these are gone, you are to come get some more."

"But I can't accept . . ."

"Let me give you some insight into my beloved father-in-law. He was a General during the War. However, even if there never had been a war, he would have been a General. I think you understand what I mean. When he says you are to come get some more greens, just consider it an order. That is the safest approach for all concerned."

Mrs. Wilhite left the dresses and the greens and headed back to Catalpa.

*   *   *

Momma Mae's panfried steak seemed tastier than ever this evening. Given the unexpected nature of Mr. Weiberg's visit this morning, the day's schedule got crammed into a small piece of the afternoon. There had been no time for lunch. I hoped that I could get past supper without the endless questions from my sisters. The meal started off easy enough. Grandpa and my father exchanged reports on their respective days. As close as they were, they found it best that they supervise different aspects of the business. The General was the herd master, keeping tabs on bulls, cows, and calves. My father was more focused on forages. Therefore, it was natural that he also accept responsibility for the sharecroppers. The General wanted nothing to do with cotton, cotton growers, or cotton problems.

My mother waited until the men had finished talking, then she spoke.

"Did you know that the Weibergs are living in an old tattered Confederate tent?"

The question seemed to be launched in the general direction of the two adult males, but neither one gave any indication that they cared to reply.

Undeterred, she proceeded, "I mean, they are just camping out. They have nothing to wear. It is just wretched."

The General swallowed hard before he spoke. "Devon, does that surprise you? The entire South is bankrupt. Everyone is starting over, some with nothing, some with little more than nothing."

"Well, I think I could get some of the ladies at church to contribute some clothing and maybe some food to help these folks out."

"These folks," the General repeated. "Now, just who might 'these folks' be?"

"Well, the Weibergs. The ladies could adopt them . . ."

"Just the Weibergs. How convenient, Devon. When you went out there today, did you spend any time visiting with Mrs. Weiberg?"

"Yes, sir, we had a little talk."

"Did she seem the type of person who wanted to accept charity?"

"Well, no, sir."

"Do you think she would want it known that she's now a ward of a bunch of church ladies who know exactly what she needs?"

"No, sir, but she needs so much."

"And what would you start with—food, clothing, or a new plow? How about a good mule?"

"I don't know, but . . ."

"Luther, how many croppers do we have down in the bottom right now?"

"I would have to say thirty or so."

"And how many came off this plantation?"

"Everyone but Weiberg and two families from another plantation in Grimes County."

"So, Devon, you have selected the only white sharecropper family in the Catalpa bottom. What do your church ladies plan to do
with the other twenty-nine families?"

"Sir, you know as well as I do that those ladies probably wouldn't
be interested in helping any of the Negroes."

"Here is what I know. I know that every Sunday the churches
of Monaville are filled with the largest assembly of hypocrites this
county has ever seen. They congregate to be seen for the simple purpose of convincing one another that, in short order, they shall be
resurrected as saints sitting with the archangels themselves. Should
they undertake any charitable action during the middle of the
week, it is solely for their own self-aggrandizement. It gives them
the chance to stand on a stump and look down at the rest of the
world while they pass judgment on all who are below them. I know
this from firsthand experience, I know it well, and I have known it
for years. Your church ladies of Monaville are not welcome on this
plantation, now or ever.

"Second, if I am any judge of character, Mr. Weiberg is a proud,
hardworking individual who is not inclined to accept charity. I can
help him in some ways and would be happy to do so. But I shall not
rob him or anyone else of his dignity.

"Last, we already have an element here in our beloved community that wants to rewrite history. Devon, we lost the War. All those
croppers that I used to own are now citizens. They can vote. I can't
because I fought for the CSA. Yet, the church ladies are not so
charitable toward them. I have no idea how things will end up, but
until I figure it out, I will cut square corners with everyone, and I

mean everyone, until they prove not worthy. As poor as all of those croppers are, they had better be prepared to help one another when it comes time to pick that cotton. If the Weibergs are the sole beneficiaries of your charity, I doubt that they will get much help from their neighbors.

"Now, that's enough about sharecroppers. I'm going to bed."

My parents sat quietly at the table while Grandpa went upstairs. This was more conversation than I was prepared for, and it had covered a lot of territory and raised all kinds of questions. While it might be a little dangerous, I thought one question wouldn't hurt.

"Pa, why doesn't Grandpa go to church?"

"John Ross, there is more to that question than you will ever know. You are old enough and smart enough to guess from this conversation that the church ladies are a part of it. However, there is a lot of history that you will learn in due time."

Another less-than-satisfying answer. Grown-ups are sure riddles. I think I'll continue my research with Blue.

CHAPTER 3

The Great Turtle Roundup

AFTON DECIDED TO RAISE turtles. Personally, I never had much interest in turtles. Momma Mae would occasionally make turtle soup. It was fair enough, but it paled next to her other recipes.

Somehow, Afton had hoodwinked me into rowing her down the Brazos to collect turtles. She was not going to be content with just one kind of turtle. No, for land sakes, she wanted one of every type we could find—red eared, shedders, mud turtles, box turtles, snapping turtles, plus maybe some soft-shelled ones. But in all honesty, I didn't mind spending time with Afton.

Years earlier, she was just another kid. While there were some things I considered fun that she didn't, she pretty much enjoyed everything everyone else enjoyed.

Now, though, she was different—a little more reserved, seeming to understand things I really didn't understand. Her shape had softened. Bony, angular body parts were becoming rounder and softer. If it were not for all the talk about my "friend" Afton, I could get used to spending a whole lot more time with her. For now, this girl was on a mission—to round up every turtle we could find.

First, I had to get past Afton's mother. My pa once told me that when you like a girl, take a good look at her mom because that is what she would eventually look like. That was the rub. Her mom was nice enough—reserved and generally pleasant. But she was a mud hen for sure. You just had to wonder how Afton could have turned out so good-looking.

She was sitting in the buggy when I arrived.

"Why are you in that buggy, Afton?"

"Well, I can't tie the turtles to my horse, silly. If I did, neither I nor the turtles or the horse would get home in one piece."

I suppose she had a point. "Good Lord, how many turtles are we shootin' for?"

"All we can get."

Somehow I kind of knew that would be her answer. So off we headed for the river. Just south of town, there was a low spot in the bank. An old skiff was tied there . . . sort of a town asset, if you will. If no one was using it, we could get downriver with it and maybe onto some of the sandbars. There was only one problem. The shortest route was straight through the middle of town.

"Let's take the Oakridge road."

"Why, John Ross? That's way out of the way. We would just be burning daylight. We'll go through town."

She snapped the reins and off she went as if that was the last word. And, apparently, it was. I followed her into town, which was precisely her point. The closer we got to town, the more agitated I got.

"Afton, how about if you go through town and I just come around through the alley?"

"Why? Are you ashamed of me?"

"Well, no."

"Then, what?"

"I just don't want to be following your buggy like a puppy dog."

"John Ross, you're silly."

"No, I'm not. Let me ride in front."

"Oh, so I'll be the puppy dog. I think not."

We went through Monaville side by side, which may have been worse. It seemed that every old bag in the county was out that day, pointing, grinning, and smiling. Didn't these women have something better to do? I could at least resume a normal breathing pattern once we got out of town.

The skiff was there. Afton and I loaded it with some boxes to hold our treasure trove of turtles. To my surprise, Afton had a picnic basket, which both delighted and confused me.

"We going picnicking?"

"I figured we would eat the fried chicken and use the bones to catch more turtles."

"Well, you are certainly resourceful."

The river was fairly low and moving slowly. In places, it was best to hug the bank.

"Afton, you aren't interested in starting a collection of water moccasins are you? 'Cause I suspect that we'll see a few on some of these low-lying branches."

Picking up the extra oar, she poked it at my chest twice. "You let any snakes fall into this boat and you're a dead man."

I grinned. "Now, Afton, you forget, I'm in the boat too."

We found a good place to land—good in the sense that we could get out of the skiff without getting our feet wet. However, it wasn't short of green briars or berry brambles. I cut a couple of sticks to help us lift the brush and ward off any snakes, skunks, or other critters that might inadvertently crash Afton's turtle roundup.

Much to my surprise, it didn't take long to gather a couple of box turtles and a few softshells. Afton thought it best to stop the hunt and start the picnic, which suited me just fine. I suspected she wanted the bones so we could go after the big game out on the sandbar.

We found a high-and-dry spot under a post oak tree. Afton had filled that basket with food. We started on the sliced cinnamon apples, while Afton explained this whole turtle-farming concept to me. Apparently, more folks liked turtle soup than I had really appreciated. Her idea was to figure out which turtles she could domesticate and sell. Personally, I had never given a passing thought to domesticating a turtle, but if she kept fixing the picnic baskets, she could domesticate a whole lot more than turtles.

"Oh! Dale, you scared me."

I turned to see the source of Afton's surprise, but you could usually smell Dale before you could see him. He had gone off to the War with the other Monaville men as their drummer. He didn't have much family. The menfolk were all he had. They were glad to have him and he was glad just to belong. But that was during an exciting time when the War was still a jubilation. The reality of it would soon come crashing down on all of them.

Dale never attended school. No hovering mother insisted on his attendance. He was slow talking and slow walking. It was anyone's guess whether that was caution or just ignorance dressed up like caution.

He quickly learned that the South needed fewer drummer boys and more soldiers. So, he participated in every engagement with the General and the other Monaville men, acting most often as the

General's runner. General Wilhite had hoped that such a youngster would be spared some of the violence and carnage. However, in the end, no one was spared the grisly destruction of the South.

Dale didn't return with the rest of the men; well, not directly anyway. Dale became the hermit on the Brazos River, as he came to be known in Monaville. During the summer, he lived in the bottomland, surviving on berries, fish, and Afton's soon-to-be-domesticated turtles.

When the river rose during the fall and winter, he moved to higher ground. But usually, he stayed on the river, never entering into town much.

Dale looked starved. The shell-shocked look had never left him. Most veterans had gradually lost that faraway look of shock and fear. Sometimes, they would experience its return for brief intermittent spells, but it never left Dale.

"Howdy, Afton. Howdy, John Ross. Didn't mean to scare you."

"That's no problem, Dale. John Ross and I are just starting. Would you like to join us?"

"I would be lyin' if I said no."

Afton offered Dale the cinnamon apples, which I knew Dale needed more than I did. However, I hated to see them go.

"John Ross, how is the General?"

"He is fine, sir."

"I used to see him on his bay horse down in the bottoms, but now I see your father more than the General."

"Pa is taking care of the croppers now and Grandpa spends his time with the herd . . . and his horses."

"Oh yes, the General does like his horses. He's still quite a sight on horseback. Just to see him used to calm me so."

Dale ate his way through the food in Afton's picnic basket, all the while inquiring about his former fellow soldiers. Once the empty interior of the basket was completely visible to us all, Dale thanked Afton and, as quickly and quietly as he had arrived, he left. It was difficult not to want to share the food with someone who was in desperate need of it. However, I felt some resentment over the intrusion, a befuddling emotion. I had my suspicions, but I didn't want to think about them too long. My long-standing relationship with Afton seemed to be taking some unusual twists and turns.

"John Ross, why doesn't Dale live in town, or for that matter, anywhere but these bottoms?"

"I expect he's more comfortable here."

"But he knows all the men in town, surely someone could put him to work."

"Oh, I don't think Dale is one bit lazy. I guess he likes it here."

"Did he just take up living on the river when all the men came home?"

"Yes. Well, no."

"Which is it? Yes or no?"

"Dale didn't come home with the men. In fact, as I understand it, he arrived sooner than the rest and had already taken to living here."

"You mean he deserted?"

"I don't know. I've overheard some of the men talk. Toward the end of the War, there was no food. It was clear to all that the South would lose. Some just left. I guess that's what he did. Although, it's funny, I haven't ever heard my grandpa say anything about it."

"He doesn't look in real good health."

"No, he doesn't. Camping out is fun, but you get over it quickly. Living on the river, it's got to be tough."

"Maybe I should make another picnic basket."

"Afton, I would never want to discourage you, or anyone, from bringing a picnic lunch. Especially if I am likely to get some of the fixin's. But I just heard a whole lot of talk at our table about offering people charity. Perhaps you ought to sleep on the idea."

"Let me guess, I bet your grandpa had a whole lot to say about that."

"True, he did, but that doesn't mean you shouldn't give it some thought."

Afton turned to pack the basket and gather her things. I took this to mean that the picnic part of the trip was over. Her last comment was confusing. Afton had never spent any time with my grandpa. In fact, he seldom left Catalpa since returning from the War. She obviously had formed her opinion from afar. I had some vague idea that there was a connection between all these thoughts of charity and Grandpa's recent admonitions about churchgoing ladies. Afton's mom was in the first pew every Sunday.

The rest of the day was hard labor. Afton could spot, or think she saw, far more turtles than I could catch. The sandbars were far and away the most heavily populated hunting ground.

However, Afton wanted more variety. This encouraged us—me—to explore the brambles and briars that were dense along the banks. Fortunately, we accosted no snakes. By day's end, we had over thirty turtles that refused to stay still long enough for an accurate head count.

Our return trip through Monaville provoked the same anxiety in me as our first trip, but it was close to dusk and the types of inhabitants visible on the street were significantly different now. These folks were focused on finding a drink at Nuncio's or perhaps a little more. They showed no interest in us.

CHAPTER 4

Questions and Some Answers

"MORNIN', BLUE."

"Mornin', John Ross."

Blue was dripping sweat. It was a tombstone day and he had already been hard at it. The stone was Sarah Weiberg's. The name and dates were finished and he had sketched a small angel on the limestone block.

"Did the Weibergs want that angel, Blue?"

"No, thought I'd add it. I just hates to see a young person die. You thinks dey would mind me addin' it?"

"Mind? I can't imagine they would mind. They'd probably really like it."

I figured I'd see the final product when Blue set the stone. I had ducked out of the funeral. They just weren't my favorite pastime. The preacher had seemed really wound up. I feared he would go on forever. I have often wondered whether they thought they were really helping. Every time he mentioned Sarah's name, Mrs. Weiberg would let out another moan, and her tears would flow again. It seemed to me, preachers ought to be quick about it. Say a few words and let the family get on with grieving on their own. This preacher talked like he knew Sarah, which wasn't possible. Anyway, during a moment of high emotion, I made my escape.

"John Ross, dey say you and Afton came through town yesterday."

His "dey" meant the entire population of Monaville was discussing my infernal ride through town.

"Yes, Blue, we went turtle hunting down on the river."

"Find any?"

"Oh, yeah, caught a bunch on the sandbars."

"Oh, da sandbars. I spent lots of time down dere as a kid with your grandpa, my sister Elisabeth, Colonel Whitworth, Big Charlie, and Miss Hightower . . . I think every child in da Brazos River bottom played dere. Is dat big rope still there?"

"I didn't notice any rope."

"Probably rotted away. I forgets how old I am. Dere was a huge oak tree on da bank. Didn't have many low limbs. Somehow, Big Charlie climbed to one of da high branches and tied da rope up dere. We had fun swinging out over da river, trying to drop off in da water and not hit da sandbar. Course dose sandbars moves and it got tricky."

"Can't see Miss Hightower doing anything fun. Now that I think of it, can't see Grandpa doing anything fun. They both are so serious."

"Life makes you serious, John Ross. We all starts out as chil'ren with nothin' but fun on our mind."

"Big Charlie would certainly be the one to climb the tree."

"Big Charlie was always big, but back then, he was skinny. Whoa, dat boy was skinny."

"How about Colonel Whitworth? I bet he wasn't skinny."

"Not as thin as Big Charlie. But there wasn't much meat on any of us . . . 'cept me; I always been round."

Blue laughed and seemed to drift off, thinking about the innocent time of his childhood.

"You never speak of your sister, Elisabeth. Where is she?"

In an instant, Blue's entire demeanor changed. The hammer and chisel dropped to his side. Blue's focus was on the ground at his feet. I had raised a topic that I now wished I hadn't.

"She was kilt, John Ross, kilt," Blue said with emotion.

"I'm sorry. I didn't know."

"John Ross, are you ready to rent the courtin' carriage? Popular opinion in Monaville says you are. I can make you a deal."

Neither Blue nor I had noticed that Colonel Whitworth had slipped into the barn. How long he had been there was anybody's guess.

"Yes, sir, I mean, no, sir . . . at least not now." Colonel Whitworth had a way of asking me questions that called for answers I just didn't have or didn't know.

"Hop in this buggy of mine. These horses seem to need a little harness work. I would like your opinion."

Colonel Whitworth hadn't asked me to ride with him in years. It seemed like an odd request, but one that I should honor.

"Just head them out north of town." I guided them as directed, but once out of Blue's earshot the Colonel turned to me.

"John Ross, there ain't a damn thing in the world wrong with these horses or their harness, or if there is, I'm not smart enough to know it. I thought Blue might want a moment to himself . . . to compose himself. Whether you know it or not, your question wandered right into some painful memories for Blue."

"I feel so bad. I never knew much about his sister, much less that she was killed."

"Oh, hell. I know that. No way that you would or even should. Blue and Elisabeth were real close . . . only a year apart. Well, we all were close."

"But . . ."

"Yes, I know. It was slave times. I know what you're thinking. But when younguns are younguns, that's all they are—just younguns. The slave quarters weren't a hundred feet from the main house on any plantation anywhere. Hell, on some of the smaller farms, the slaves slept under the porch. Those slave families were procreating as fast as the white families."

"Procreating, sir?"

"Reproducing, John Ross . . . having babies. Let me put it this way. You like horses, right?"

"Yes, sir."

"In fact, you're very good with them. But where did you get the idea? I suspect it was from your father and grandfather, both being fond of horses."

"I suppose."

"So when we were young, we learned by watching the grown-ups. I learned how to plant cotton. Big Charlie learned how to grow cotton. Blue learned how to be a blacksmith. Don't ask me how he developed that gravestone, grave, and graveyard business because I sure as hell don't know. Anyway, the vast majority of us kids just followed in our parents' footsteps. To be sure, I guess the white kids had a good many more options. The Negroes were going to be slaves. But within the framework that existed at the time, we all just gradually found our niche. But we all started out playing in the same damn mud hole. The one unspoken secret that no one will admit is that we all know we started in the same mud hole."

"Colonel Whitworth, who killed Blue's sister?"

"A Catalpa slave named Rack, the meanest son of a bitch I have ever known."

"They were both slaves at the plantation?"

"That's right."

"How did it happen?"

"John Ross, let's leave it at that for now. You are a bright young man. Undoubtedly, there will be a time when you will know or should know the whole story. In Monaville, you will pick up bits from time to time like so many pieces to a puzzle. I will make you this promise. When you have a question about something, come see me. If I think you are ready for the answer, I'll tell you. If I think you aren't, I promise you that I will tell you when I think you're ready. That's as fair as I can be. There is a lot of history in this old river bottom—some good, some bad, some forgotten, and some that ought to be forgotten. But if you're going to live here, and I suspect you are, then you're going to have to deal with it. I don't have kids and you are the grandson of my best friend, albeit a poor choice I must admit. So I will try to piece things together for you when I can. Fair enough?"

"Yes, sir. I can ask you questions and if you think I'm ready to know the answer, you'll tell me."

"That's right."

"Well, would it be all right to start today?"

"Something tells me that you have a warehouse full of stored-up questions. Let's go ahead and wade into it."

"Mr. Weiberg's daughter died."

"Yes, I heard."

"My mother wanted to get some of her friends from church together and . . ."

"Don't say any more. Adopt the Weibergs, feed them, take care of them, and do all sorts of good deeds for them?"

"Yes, sir. Grandpa said there wasn't going to be any church ladies on Catalpa."

"And your question is why would General Leander Wilhite stomp on the good intentions of the fine church ladies of Monaville in the same fashion he would stomp out a prairie fire or a Yankee insurrection?

"I can answer that on a couple of levels, but first, I must swear you to secrecy. My dear wife, who I love very much, is probably the exact person Leander had in mind when he said 'church ladies.' God only knows that woman is more than just a little bit involved in church work. So we'll keep this talk between us."

"Yes, sir."

"First, the church ladies are a group of elitists who look for reasons to look down on everyone and one another, including a poor sharecropper like Mr. Weiberg and his family. So all the good deeds really are designed to reinforce their idea that somehow, some way, they are better than the rest of the world. You understand that much?"

"Sort of."

"The long and short of it is that if they want to help the Weibergs, why do they need to do it as a group? Every one of those women can drive a buggy. They could just head out with whatever they want to give the Weiberg family. That isn't what they want to do. They want to discuss, organize, and make it complicated. They want an audience, particularly one that they care about and can impress.

"Next, it is odd that they picked one of the few white sharecroppers around. John Ross, I don't know how this world of ours is going to get sorted out, or if it ever will. I do know that folks who might not have rubbed shoulders before the War may have to learn how to get along with folks they may not like. Before the War, slaves were at the bottom of the pecking order. Now it's a real good question who is on the bottom.

"Catalpa and Oakridge Plantations never borrowed money on their land. That's why they are still in one piece. A lot of cotton growers, big and small, did and are now sharecroppers or damn close. Hell, our drunken Sheriff M. E. Brown is burning furniture just to keep warm. He and others will soon find their land owned by Mr. T. Roliff Harrington III . . . the thieving Yankee bastard. What I'm saying is that the Weibergs are going to need help to make a go of their crop. Becoming the pet of a bunch of church ladies will not work to their benefit.

"Last, our good General hates church ladies, and I suspect most church men. He feels they are hypocrites who seldom, if ever, practice what they preach. Fortunately, he does make some allowance for some of us married men who attend on Sunday so that our ladies are more, shall we say, agreeable during the rest of the week. Given some of the innuendos that have been floated his way, I can't say as I blame him. Once again, this is one of those grand areas with a great deal of history to it. However, I would not be too critical of your grandfather. He has more than enough justification to feel the way he does. Any more questions?"

"Not right now, sir."

"Good. In that case, I have a business proposition for you. Are you interested in making a little money?"

"Yes, sir!"

"I haven't got all the facts yet, but when I do, I'll need you to drop what you're doing because time will be very limited."

"Sure. What will I be doing?"

"Nothing illegal, John Ross, but for now I have to keep things close to my vest. Are you at Blue's every morning?"

"Every morning that's a school day. And even on weekends I generally show up."

"That's good. I know where to find you, plus you can learn a lot from Blue. I am sure he enjoys your company."

By this time, we had circled the town and were fast approaching Blue's.

"When you go back into the barn, just act like everything is normal. I am sure Blue has composed himself by now, although he might be a tad embarrassed."

"I understand, sir."

"Good. I will be back in touch. Now run along and do give my best to the General."

CHAPTER 5

Calving Season

"WELL, I HAVE TO HAND IT TO YOU, AFTON."

"Hand me what?"

"That was pretty clever, hoodwinking me into that turtle roundup, so you could use turtle domestication as your science project."

"I did no such thing, Mr. Wilhite! I didn't know anything about any science project. Anyway, I am serious about my turtle project."

A little anger brought some color to her cheeks, which made her cuter than usual, if that was possible. I decided to continue provoking Afton.

"No doubt you are a good deal more serious now that old Scarecrow Hightower has approved it for your semester grade."

"If you are so put out about it, maybe she would let us work on it together."

Now this thoroughly confused me and called for faster thinking and a quicker response than I was prepared to give. There was no doubt that spending more time with Afton would be fun. But

I wasn't certain how much science I would learn and, whenever Afton and I appeared in the same hemisphere, there was always gossip. For now, I just exercised my male prerogative to be stubborn.

"I don't think so. I believe it is a little unfair of someone who gets paid to teach to assign us all this work to do on our own. For the past year and a half, we have done nothing but one project after another."

"But, John Ross, haven't you learned things from those projects?"

"Yes, but I'm growing weary of projects."

"I think you're growing weary of answering to a female." Sometimes Afton could surprise me. "Maybe you ought to give her a list of projects you would like to do."

"Maybe I will." Though, for the life of me, I couldn't think of a single one.

We were turning onto the Oakridge-Catalpa road, gradually descending toward the Brazos River bottom. Our horses seemed a bit anxious. The sky was overcast for an afternoon, but I didn't see anything terribly foreboding.

From our elevation, all you could see was miles of cotton plants. To be sure, they were now a quilt of small patches. No continuous rows as in slave times. However, about the same amount of land was still under cultivation. What was terribly different now was the degree of quality among the individual fields.

It wasn't hard to pick out cotton grown by Big Charlie on his plot or any of the plots he owned or leased. Without question, his was the best. He knew how to grow it and was still growing it in the same fields his ancestors had plowed.

The Weiberg plot appeared to be doing as well as most. It was certainly better than most of the croppers who were not from this area. Ocy McCoy and several of his relatives had a good bit of land leased. However, they planted late and their crop would be marginal if it made it at all.

"Afton, have you noticed something odd?"

"Like what?"

"Every field out there has kids our age working in it, but I've never seen one of them in school. I guess Old Lady Hightower's reputation has gotten around."

"I doubt that it has anything to do with Miss Hightower. They are all working just to survive."

"I don't like picking cotton, but I'm not growing very fond of more school, either."

"Be careful what you wish for, John Ross."

The horses were getting restless. The wind had shifted and was blowing from the east. Most of our weather comes out of the south during the summer and the north during the winter. We don't get much weather out of the east, and when we do, it is generally bad.

The sky kept growing darker rapidly from the east, leaving a brighter sky out to the west. As the wind picked up, the temperature dropped quickly. We suddenly felt a painful chill, followed by huge drops of rain. The rain didn't fall in sheets; it was being hurled at us in single, large drops.

We were gradually climbing out of the bottom and directly into a fierce thunderstorm.

"Oh, crap!"

"John Ross, you need to watch your language, young man."

I heard the young man part but immediately spurred my horse in the direction of our heifer pasture. Grandpa had chosen this field for calving. It was close to the bottom and would grow enough grass for heifer and calf. However, that wasn't the only reason Grandpa selected it. Since he started his daily ride at the far reaches of Catalpa and gradually worked his way home, he would cross this pasture about midday. Situated where it was, I would pass it every weekday morning and evening as I went to and from school.

The Appaloosa wasted no time in getting where I wanted her to go. I glanced back hoping that Afton was following my lead. She was only about 50 yards behind me.

In the middle of the pasture was a slight draw, sloping toward the river. And that's where I found the heifer lying headfirst, pointed slope down, struggling to give birth to her calf. She must have been at it a while. She had worn all the grass away kicking and rolling in order to move her calf down the birth canal. It was obvious she was exhausted. She didn't even try to get up or run from me and my galloping horse. The calf was still in the birth canal. The calf's nostrils were all that showed for all her pushing. Something was wrong. The calf was too big or the birth canal too small.

Rain was still coming down, but I hardly noticed. At least it cooled the heifer. The sky was now dark gray and offered a brilliant lightning display that, so far, was moving horizontally across the horizon.

"Afton, can you ride toward the house and get my grandpa? He should be in the old hay meadow about a mile and a half farther down the road. I think I'm going to need some help. This heifer isn't making much progress at all."

"Me? Get the General? I don't know . . ."

"What's the problem? Just tell him I need help with a downed heifer."

"But John Ross, I don't know that I have spoken to the General in years, if ever."

"Afton!"

"I mean, he is the General."

"Afton, he doesn't bite. I can't do much for this heifer without some help. All I have in my saddlebags are some damn schoolbooks and this heifer can't read. Now, get!"

She must have gotten the message. Starting off slowly at first, she was moving quickly by the time she hit the road. Whatever fear she had of my grandpa was outweighed by her affection for any critter on four legs.

It took about four terrific thunderclaps with accompanying lightning bolts for them to return. The storm was pretty fierce. Females always seemed to choose the best weather for birthdays. This girl even selected a natural floodway with her head pointed downstream. My grandpa rode up close and took in the situation from horseback.

"John Ross, I don't think we should tie her. She's worn out, and we will need her to stand."

"Yes, sir." I was feeling a little better just having him here. This was a pretty nice heifer. If she was going to lose her calf or worse, I preferred that Grandpa have a hand in it as well.

"Afton, please hand these strips of rawhide to John Ross."

Now that floored me. I can't recall if Afton had ever met my grandpa. He certainly hadn't seen her in years. Apparently they had made quick introductions during the ride back

Both strips of rawhide, retrieved from his saddlebags, were about three-and-a-half feet in length.

"Now, John Ross, clear any of that membrane away from the calf's nostrils. We don't want it to cause a problem once the calf moves on out. Now, push the head back in."

"Back in?"

"Yes, don't worry. The calf is still buttoned to its momma. Sometimes it's best to start from the beginning. Now, can you feel the two front feet?"

"Yes, sir."

"Are they pointed down like they are supposed to?"

"Yes, sir."

"Half hitch a piece of this rawhide just above the first knuckle on each leg. You may have to pull one leg out at a time."

This was slow work. It was dark. I was working inside a heifer and had to time my movements to match the illumination of the lightning. By now, we were screaming at each other in order to be heard over the rain and thunder. With strips of hide tied to each leg, I looked up at Grandpa.

"How's she breathing?"

"Just regular, I guess."

"Good. Don't do anything. If she is breathing slowly that means you can relax. Now, watch her sides. When she takes a deep breath, you pull on one rawhide strip. Then, when she takes another deep breath, pull on the other strip. We are going to work the calf out one leg at a time. Pull straight out for now."

I was worried about pushing the calf back in. Right now I barely had two front hooves showing. I had just glanced away when Grandpa hollered to pull one leg. Sure enough, the heifer's sides had swollen up and the contraction was strong. Pulling on the right rawhide strip, the leg moved slowly out. The heifer started breathing rapidly.

"Now, stop, John Ross. Get a hold of the other strip and wait."

This time I wasn't going to look off. Grandpa might tolerate one lapse of concentration, but not two.

The second contraction was stronger than the first. I guess she saw some hope at unburdening herself of this rather large blockage.

Right and left. Right and left we went. The same progress was made. We now had two full legs out and most of the nose.

"Keep pulling the legs straight out until you get to the midtorso of the calf."

The heifer was starting to take more of an interest in this procedure. Periodically, she would lift her head to look at me. This made me think that not tying her down wasn't such a good idea after all, but I continued to pull one rawhide strip at a time.

"John Ross, move your butt down toward her feet. You're about halfway there. Now, I want you to twist that calf's torso a little so that it's at an angle. Pull the calf down, not straight out. If she were standing, you would be pulling at an angle toward the ground. Not a severe angle, but a gradual angle."

It wasn't hard for me to move in the mud. I just slid over a couple feet.

I waited for the next contraction. This time, much to my surprise, the rest of the calf literally popped out, afterbirth and all.

"Press on his rib cage a little." The calf coughed. His lungs were filled with a good deal of fluid, but he was breathing on his own. Through the now lightly falling rain, I could see that he was a pretty good-sized bull calf—large enough to give any heifer a problem.

The heifer rolled slightly and then struggled to get to her feet. Slick mud and her position downhill made this a problem.

"John Ross, pass this lariat rope under her front quarter and tie it to your saddle horn." As she struggled, Grandpa and I backed our horses away, giving her just enough lift to get her front end up. Once she was on her feet, we just dropped the rope to the ground.

"John Ross, pull the calf over to that flat place. We don't want him or his momma headed downhill, or downstream, for that matter."

I removed the rawhide from the calf's legs. He seemed genuinely pleased to be here. The heifer waited until I moved away, then she started licking away the membrane while making her own grunts and groans. Those sounds would bind her calf to her from now on. "John Ross, I'll stay here with the heifer for a while. You had better get Afton home. I am sure her parents are concerned. Afton, I thank you for getting me."

"Oh, that was quite all right, sir."

To be truthful, I was pretty well spent. I had done more pulling than I realized. However, we made it back to the road and to Afton's house. Of course, when I needed the rain most, it stopped. I was covered in mud, blood, afterbirth, and cow shit. I must have been a terrible sight judging from the look on Afton's mom's face.

"Mom, you probably don't recognize 'Dr. Wilhite,' our new vet. We just came from emergency surgery where Dr. Wilhite saved another life."

"I'm sorry we're late, ma'am, we had a heifer down."

"John Ross," said Afton, "it looks to me like you got your science project topic."

"I do? What?"

"Emergency techniques of calf delivery."

Sometimes she could be so cute and so aggravating at the same time.

CHAPTER 6

Cotton

"JOHN ROSS? JOHN ROSS? JOHN ROSS? WHERE IS THAT BOY?"

The last John Ross was almost downright operatic. Colonel Whitworth was in a high state of dudgeon. I was one of those lucky Southern boys who always had the pleasure of being called by my first and middle name. For most kids, those without my rank, the middle name was employed only when a certain level of anger had been reached. If, on occasion, the same level of wrath was directed at me, the salutation became John Ross Wilhite. This gave me sufficient warning so that I knew to answer promptly or leave the county—my choice.

Today, I answered Colonel Whitworth before my surname became involved.

"Yes, sir, I'm in here."

Colonel Whitworth's pigeon-toed feet made quick tracks for the tack room of Blue's barn.

"Today's the day, John Ross. Yes, it is the day."

"The day for what, sir?"

"The day you go to work for me. Remember our conversation?"

I had some vague recollection of a discussion with the Colonel. However, a lot had happened since then—the great turtle roundup, me becoming almost a vet, and other matters of equal distinction.

"You need to saddle up that half-baked Injun pony of yours and go tack these flyers up on every crossroad in the county. This has to get done right now. I have no idea how long old Cotton is going to stay around."

"Cotton? Who's Cotton?"

"Jesus, boy, didn't your grandpa ever tell you anything? Cotton is a white buffalo. He hasn't been seen around here for years. He's old as hell, but I think we can still have some fun with him."

"What kind of fun do you have with a buffalo?" I had to admit that my knowledge of buffalo was sketchy at best. There couldn't be more than a couple hundred left in the entire state of Texas.

"We're going to have a ropin', or at least we're going to try."

I cut a glance over in Blue's direction, having my personal doubts about anyone's ability to rope something that was larger than most of the horses ridden in these parts. Blue seemed quietly bemused by the Colonel, like somehow he had traveled this road before and wasn't interested in repeating the experience but wouldn't mind seeing a few others give it a try.

"Colonel, you mean you expect to actually see someone rope and tie this buffalo?"

"Oh, hell no. Frankly, I don't care if they do or don't. I just want to handle the wagering. And no, they don't have to tie ol' Cotton. They just have to get a rope on him."

That didn't seem that hard—just lasso 'em. I had been around the good Colonel long enough to know there was a trick in it somewhere.

"Now, John Ross, you need to get after it—time's a wastin'. I figure we'll kick this party off at the Oakridge bottom about noon Saturday. That will give time for word to spread. I'm feedin' Cotton sweet feed by the ton. Or, better said, he is eating it by the ton. I suspect he'll stay in the bottom until Saturday." With that, he handed me a saddlebag filled with flyers, a hammer, and tacks.

"Now, get. You're my partner in this deal." He disappeared as quickly as he had arrived.

"Blue, what do you know about this buffalo-ropin' business?"

"Not much, John Ross. If it's da same white buffalo, he showed up here before da War."

"Did anyone rope him?"

"No one dat I knows."

I spent the rest of the day and early evening traveling all the main roads around Monaville. Wherever there was a crossroad, I nailed up a flyer in the most prominent place I could find. Wherever I found someone heading to another town, I gave them some flyers and tacks. Coming back through Monaville, I saw that Colonel Whitworth had almost wallpapered every bulletin board in town. Gathering from the flyer and conversations I had with folks who saw it, this could be quite an event.

Supposedly, a white buffalo was sacred to the Indians. When it returned, the Indians would take back their land from the white man. To me, it seemed like the horse had already gotten out of that barn and they were just looking at the rear end of the same animal.

The Colonel wasn't going to let Cotton's return be wasted. From what I could figure, the rules were fairly simple. You paid Colonel Whitworth ten dollars to enter the contest. Old Cotton apparently didn't have to pay anything. You had ten minutes to lasso the buffalo, just lasso him. If you were successful, there was a hundred dollars in prize money coming to you. It was anybody's guess whether old Cotton knew the rules.

The next day, the Colonel seemed in grand spirits. The boys at Nuncio's tavern were signing up and some had even paid the entrance fee. Word had spread and several groups were planning to come to Oakridge for the ropin'. The simplicity of the contest had certainly gotten my interest. I was fairly good at roping. I had never lassoed anything as big as a buffalo, but the Appaloosa was quick, and I seldom missed a yearling, which had to be harder to rope than an old buffalo of questionable vintage. The Indians hunted with the same kind of horse I was riding. What was the trick? A hundred dollars was a huge temptation.

After school, I ran my thoughts by Afton. Being a female and totally uninterested in contests of any sort, I figured she would see what I was missing. But she offered little to no encouragement.

"John Ross, why would you want to do it?" was her only response.

Apparently, her female brain had failed to regard the idea of one hundred dollars in prize money. Even ignoring that part, why wouldn't I want to do it? We made no headway on the issue.

"John Ross, everyone knows Colonel Whitworth is a world-class character. It just can't be on the level."

Now, she had a point. As generous as he had been to his people, Colonel Whitworth wasn't known to give money away. He was a businessman, one of the few in Monaville, and he said he wanted to handle the betting. Therein may lie some clue.

"If you are so darn interested, why don't you talk to someone who knows something about buffalo?"

"Well, who would that be, Afton?"

"Find an Indian, you dummy!"

Now this really was irritating. Of course, who would know more about buffalo than an Injun? I should have figured that out myself. I'm sure it would've come to me eventually. The difficulty was that my ancestral fathers had reduced the numbers of Indians considerably.

But there was one—Broken Feather. I hadn't seen him in years, but I knew where to find him.

His name hadn't always been Broken Feather. Indians changed their names every so often, or they had their names changed for them based on some event. I imagined or at least I hoped that at some point in his earlier life he'd had some noble-sounding name—Soaring Eagle or something equally majestic. I had heard that the fallen angels of Nuncio's had given him his current name for reasons that escape me.

The last time I saw him, he was camped out under a bois d'arc tree behind Nuncio's. Given his preference for alcohol, that would be a good place to begin my search.

I hadn't been over in that direction for some time; however, nothing had changed. The same large collection of bottles still supported the back corner of the building. The pile was no bigger, but no smaller either. I assumed they eventually decomposed or someone carted them off.

There was a bump under the bois d'arc or, at a distance, what looked like a bump. As I approached, it started to look more like a horizontal Injun. Best I can remember, I don't recall ever seeing Broken Feather standing up. As my horse approached, his nostrils taking in the pungent odor of alcohol—cheap alcohol mixed with body odor at that—he exhaled loudly enough to wake the sleeping Injun.

Broken Feather wasn't too concerned about who was approaching. I guess he figured the whites had killed all the Indians they needed. He turned slowly in my direction. His hair was silver, worn in braids. His trousers were like mine, but he had a beaded strip of rawhide going down the side seams. He wore a dirty white shirt and a black vest, which seemed to be the Injun uniform of the day.

"Howdy, sir," I said, not knowing exactly what the proper salutation should be to the only known surviving member of his race . . . at least around Monaville.

"Umph," was his response.

"Sir, I am John Ross Wilhite . . ."

"Yes, I know—the General's grandson."

"Yes, sir. I have a couple of questions about buffalo, and I thought you might know the answers or could help me." I was fumbling and Afton's idea didn't seem as good as it had a while ago.

"Buffalo? Why would you want to know about buffalo?"

"Well, Colonel Whitworth . . ."

"Oh! The buffalo roping."

"Yes, sir, you've heard about it?"

He pointed toward Nuncio's. "Anyone who has spent any time in there lately knows about it."

"I'm a pretty good roper, and I'm riding a fairly quick pony, so do you think I have a chance?"

"No."

"No! Why not?"

"You white people. You think we Injuns just rode alongside a buffalo herd and took the ones we wanted."

"Didn't you?"

"I wish it were that easy. We took what the herd would let us have."

"Sir, I'm confused."

"John Ross, the buffalo on the outside of the herd aren't the best buffalo. The big bulls and prized females are in the center, protected by the weaker animals on the outside. So we killed the slower, weaker, smaller, and sicker animals. Only the crazy Comanches killed the good animals and that was by driving the whole damn herd off a cliff."

"So you don't think I can rope Cotton?"

"Cotton is the buffalo?"

"Yes, sir."

"Good that he has a name. This is the buffalo that Colonel Whitworth has been feeding in the bottom?"

"Yes, sir. I was hoping to win the hundred-dollar prize money."

"A hundred dollars is a lot of money. But there is an easier way to make a hundred dollars . . ."

"How so?"

"Bet on the buffalo."

"Bet on the buffalo?"

"Do you like that Appy you're riding?"

"Yes, sir."

"Well, use him to rope cows, not buffalo. Lots of big talk at Nuncio's. By Saturday, all those big talkers will have convinced themselves that they not only can rope a buffalo, but they could ride it too. Bet on the buffalo, and when you do, remember this old Injun because you are going to make some money."

"Thank you, thank you, sir."

I couldn't tell for sure, Broken Feather was fairly stoic like I had expected, but I thought I saw a slight smile, although I might have been mistaken. In the meantime, I thought it best to keep this conversation to myself.

Things were starting to come together. Colonel Whitworth could make a few dollars. There was no question about that. And he wanted to run the betting, so I had to figure he knew something. Plus, he was here when Cotton appeared the last time. The stuff about the weaker animals being on the outside was true enough for cattle, why not buffalo? I had seen some drawings of Indians riding alongside buffalo herds shooting arrows at them. But if they were the weaker ones, it might have been possible. Cotton was undoubtedly an old buffalo, but one Colonel Whitworth had now pumped full of sweet feed. Things were beginning to make sense.

The buffalo roping was starting to draw a crowd. By midweek, most of the locals had paid a visit to Oakridge to try and catch a glimpse of old Cotton. I could understand the simple curiosity of wanting to see a white buffalo, or for that matter, any buffalo. However, from a contestant's point of view, there wasn't much to gain from the inspection. There was nothing to compare him to. For the most part, his behavior was like that of any old bull. Yes, I confess, I made the time to see him too. Bulls graze early in the morning and late in the evening. During the heat of the day, they just lounge around under a shade tree. That is, unless there is some romancing to do. But it appeared that Cotton was alone—no girl-friends.

As buffalo go, he seemed to be a pretty fair specimen. The whiteness of his coat was not due to age. I have seen old bulls get kind of salt and pepper, sometimes giving their coat a sheen of silver. This old boy was white, which made me wonder if it was the same one that appeared some years back. The species itself was an odd contraption. It had a massive head and hump that led down to a no-count kind of ass. Even some of our rangy longhorns had more meat on their hindquarters. If your loop was big enough, you ought to be able to lasso him. There was an internal struggle going on within me. Should I take Broken Feather's advice or join in the fun?

Colonel Whitworth seemed to be moving me in the direction of Broken Feather's advice. I had been running errands and doing chores for him all week between my other errands and chores. School just got a lick and a promise. However, the Colonel paid well and seemed to be pleased with the way things were coming along.

By the time Saturday arrived, I was too darn tired to care much about this buffalo or any buffalo. There was a morning fog along the bottom, generally a good sign of rain. But the sun broke through, and folks started gathering along the hill overlooking the bottom. We had roped off an area for spectators. In theory, the contestants and Cotton were supposed to stay in the bottom and in view. Well, that was the plan.

Monaville hadn't seen such a crowd since its last public execution, which was some time ago. It was generally said that the citizens were likely to come out to kill or be killed. The "be killed" part referred to a rather notable bank robbery where some of the good citizens, armed with birdshot-loaded shotguns—it was dove season—tried to take on some desperados armed with .44s. Things didn't go well for Monaville that day.

It had never occurred to me that a buffalo ropin' was a dress-up affair. I just wore what I usually wore. The female population saw this as an event equal to a small wedding or a large funeral. The most respectable, refined, and prominent ladies, with their families in tow, quickly claimed a high point on the ground and set about arranging quilts and blankets for their comfort.

Some of the less respectable sort tried to claim an area in front of the rope until they were quickly moved to another area. Frankly, I was seeing folks I hadn't seen in years. Monaville had to be deserted. Old Blue even closed shop and meandered uphill to witness the event.

The moment I saw Colonel Whitworth, I immediately headed in his direction. I preferred this to having my name called out in front of the entire town's population. From that point on, we were pretty much joined at the hip. Don't think for a moment that a 300-pound man can't move when he wants to.

We had set up a cotton wagon as a kind of office, and contestants gradually gathered to pay their entry fees. The Colonel kept the money, and I recorded the payments. That's when the wagering began. The Colonel was extremely adept at goading some poor roper into betting on himself. After all, why would he enter and bet on the damn buffalo? I knew some of the folks and had a fair idea whether they could rope. Others, well, I just followed the Colonel's lead, putting myself down for smallish wagers.

Things were starting to settle down. The fees had been paid. The wagers made. Then it happened. Out of the corner of my eye, three wagons caught my attention. The entire crowd, which had been focused on the bottom, the buffalo, or one another, turned collectively. There was a single audible gasp, followed by total silence. It was so quiet you could hear a mouse pissing on a cotton ball.

In the first wagon was Nuncio, dressed in Mexican finery, with about six of his fallen angels seated right behind him. Dressed in silk of the harshest colors, with bosoms squeezed skyward by laced corsets, they jiggled their way in the direction of the grandstand. The second wagon held a few more soiled doves. Driving the third wagon was Broken Feather, carting enough whiskey to turn the Brazos River amber.

The Colonel grinned from ear to ear and was naturally the first to break the silence.

"Hola, Nuncio, my little friend from south of the Rio. It is good to see that someone can recognize an opportunity when he sees it."

"Hola, Colonel. Where can I set up?"

"Set up anywhere you want, just stay behind this rope."

When you listen to crowd noise, it's generally just that—crowd noise, a mixture of all kinds of voices. Initially, the crowd noise had a very female tone, as one righteous churchgoing female turned to another to murmur or say whatever churchgoing females say when coming face-to-face, or in this case bosom-to-face, with women of the evening. Then, the murmur turned masculine, as husbands tried to explain their personal willingness to run headlong up a hill toward Yankee snipers, but on no account were they going to carry the battle flag for the removal of Nuncio and his companions from this hill or any other hill.

Colonel Whitworth seemed to enjoy the consternation this turn of events had created. After some time, the Baptist preacher screwed up his courage, adjusted his tie, and marched, if preachers can be said to march, toward the Colonel.

"Colonel, what are your intentions?" To me, this seemed a rather around-the-bush start to the discussion.

"Intentions—what intentions, Reverend?"

"These women, the whiskey, the wagering. I mean, this just can't be tolerated."

"Now, that's an odd thing for you to say. Aren't you a man of the cloth?"

"Of course."

"I should think you would be in hog heaven. This old buffalo has brought you just about every sinner possible. They're all in one place, and I should think you would appreciate the convenience. You can set up shop right here."

The preacher had turned about four shades of purple as the Colonel spoke. The fact that one of the harlots called him by his first name didn't help any.

"Colonel, I demand that you stop this entire affair immediately."

"Whoa, partner. You seem a little out of sorts. Everyone was invited to this ropin', everyone. I couldn't tell who was coming and who wasn't. As far as the women and whiskey go, you're the very preacher who chose to move the Baptist church from its pastoral setting in the woods to downtown Monaville. It now rests two blocks from Nuncio's women and whiskey. As for the wagering, the entire back row of your congregation wagers every single Sunday that you couldn't possibly go on for another hour. So I can't see much difference between here and what happens in Monaville every week."

This was enough for the preacher, who returned to his congregation to the sounds of catcalls from Nuncio's crowd.

That wouldn't be the last complaint. The town seemed to be filled with men who apparently knew some of Nuncio's girls on a first-name basis. I could only gather that their wives were unaware of any relationship, speaking or otherwise, existing between their husbands and the ever-so-slightly soiled angels. I was surprised to see how many Monaville males paid a visit to the Colonel. They crossed all age groups and economic categories. Some of the poorest croppers in the valley appeared to be very good customers given the amount of grief they gave Colonel Whitworth. His reply was the same to each.

"Hell, just tell her you met her at my store. Every whore in town has to buy something from me eventually."

Those men who were too unimaginative to think of an excuse welcomed the Colonel's suggestion. The smarter ones said they would do no such thing.

In the meantime, Nuncio was doing a great business and the girls were doing everything they could to assist the sale and consumption of alcohol. Having failed to pack any tents, beds, or mattresses, they confined themselves to bartending, which gave some small comfort to the adult population—both male and female. Soon a small covey of adolescent males gathered under a tree near Nuncio's wagons. They just stared and engaged in whatever sexual fantasies their weak little minds could imagine.

I was stirred from my own daydreams by the Colonel's blowing into an old cow horn. He announced that the contest would now begin. The contestants had drawn for their positions. It was anybody's guess how long it was going to take to lasso old Cotton, assuming he *was* old and not a newer version. Therefore, whether it was better to go first and surprise him or go later when he might be tired was subject to debate.

The first roper was a darky named Napoleon Jackson from the Montgomery area. The ride to Monaville had not done Napoleon or his horse much good. Both were skin and bone. He pointed the bar of soap he was riding in the direction of the river bottom. His bony legs dangled way past the point that they should have on his undersized horse. Napoleon had a secret weapon, a bulldog of not-so-even temperament. Given the fact that there was only one rule— lasso the buffalo—the use of a dog appeared perfectly acceptable. The dog picked up the scent first, with Napoleon following not far behind him.

When Cotton heard the bark of a bulldog, he got on his feet. This drew a round of applause from the crowd. However, once the horse caught sight of the intended prey, he shied and would go no closer. Napoleon tried repeatedly to get that horse to move close enough so that he could lasso Cotton. He even tried backing him up to the buffalo. At first glance, you would think this might have merit. However, a horse can see almost completely behind himself. Therefore, no progress was made. All Cotton had to do was raise that huge head and the horse would retreat.

Colonel Whitworth blew his horn signaling that Napoleon had three minutes left to lasso the buffalo or kiss his entry fee good-bye forever. This raised a great cry from his traveling companions, who had contributed all or part of the ten dollars that was slipping away.

Jackson stopped his horse directly in front of Cotton, who had not moved very far from the shade tree he started out under. Jackson turned to that bulldog and gave him some command that was inaudible to the audience. That dog ran directly up to Cotton and did its best to nip his nose.

You had to give it to the dog. He was not intimidated by Cotton. He barked, he attacked, and retreated. He circled and attacked again. Then it happened. Cotton dropped his head slightly. Napoleon was poised on his skinny steed, lariat in hand, rocking it back and forth slightly. He knew that dog would land that hundred dollars for him. With the buffalo's head closer to the ground, the bulldog took a couple of steps and sprang at the buffalo's nose. Four incisors sunk deep into the tender tissue of Cotton's nose. Cotton gave out a deep groan. With a quick flick of his massive head, he launched that dog into the air on a collision course with the lap of one Napoleon Jackson, buffalo roper.

Napoleon and his horse couldn't move fast enough, individually or as a unit, to avoid the dog. The impact laid Jackson back against his horse's rump. The horse whirled, dropping Napoleon off one side and the dog off the other. Dog and horse headed for the canebrake at a clip they had never run before. A dazed Napoleon stood alone, looking directly into the eyes of Cotton. Being a quick learner, Napoleon called it a day and headed toward the grandstand as fast as he could. Cotton lay back down under the tree.

The next several contestants had almost the same experience. Horses were just not inclined to get near something so big that they had never seen before; you might call it "horse sense." Now that Cotton had experienced the pain that a dog could inflict, he wasn't remotely inclined to tolerate any dog's presence. In fact, the dog-versus-buffalo contest was now becoming more interesting than the man-versus-buffalo contest.

To my surprise, several contestants had brought dogs, apparently to roust or direct the buffalo. They did get the old boy to move from the shade. However, that wasn't the best part. Although he probably didn't have a lot of experience with dogs, Cotton learned quickly. He would lower his head and tilt it slightly. Protecting his nose, the woolly hair on his head was impenetrable to any bite. This gave him the opportunity to hook the dog between his head and horn and fling it. Several dogs sailed over small pine saplings. It was just amazing to watch a surprised canine cut through the air with such velocity. Cotton would then return to the shade tree, none the worse for wear.

The next featured fool was Charles McDuffie. Charles was a man of very low character and even lower taste in clothing. You see, Charles was a dude, more adept at card games than manual labor. He wore no cowboy hat, sombrero, or even surplus from the Confederate States of America. He wore an English bowler. A single bullet hole gave the hat some distinction. He told anyone who asked that it was from an errant shot fired by an irate husband. His handkerchief was as large as a small tablecloth, and it might have been one in the past, for it was checkered. His shirt was something out of the wardrobe of one of those traveling shows and would have fit best in an Elizabethan play. It was bright red and matched his checkered handkerchief. His pant legs were tucked inside his boots. He was splendid in appearance but had absolutely no utility.

He was well mounted on a barrel-chested sorrel quarter horse that had one white sock. He called him Chili. No dogs accompanied him; McDuffie was going to attack the mighty buffalo alone. The Colonel blew his horn and McDuffie rode toward his fate.

I don't know the exact provocation, or if there was one. I had turned to tabulate the bets for the Colonel. Some think it was the flowing handkerchief, which at a lope looked a little like a cape. Others say bulls, buffalo or otherwise, don't like red. Whatever it was, Cotton got up the minute McDuffie came down the hill. Cotton started to snort and paw as McDuffie rode closer.

This got the crowd's attention. Everyone was focused. By now, the crowd had divided itself into three groups. All the church ladies and their families had arrived early and claimed the high ground. It looked for all the world like a Sunday social. The freed people claimed the next hill over, slightly lower in elevation. However, since many had worked these fields, they knew that the sun would soon be at their backs, lighting the bottom with its warm intensity. In the middle area, a gradual valley, were a grand mixture of croppers, poor whites, common laborers, gamblers, riverboat men, and one or two purveyors of patented medicines. They were closest to Nuncio's wagons and seemed pretty happy. All were behind the Colonel's rope.

McDuffie stopped at the bottom of the incline to adjust his lasso. Cotton didn't wait. He headed directly toward the gallant horseman at a gallop. Hooves supporting his massive body, he thundered across the heavy soil that had grown so much cotton for so long. He didn't seem to even breathe. He just snorted. The space between

McDuffie and Cotton had narrowed more rapidly than I could've ever imagined. Of course, I had never seen a buffalo run before. McDuffie seemed unaware of how fast Cotton was approaching. At the last possible moment, McDuffie looked up and whirled his horse sideways as the buffalo sailed past him.

Returning to his senses, McDuffie looked toward the crowd, while Cotton made a huge turn and headed back toward him. Generally, you lasso something running alongside or in front of you, not something that is coming directly at you. Anyway, at the rate he was going, the buffalo would soon punch a hole in horse and rider. McDuffie must have come to the same conclusion when he saw Cotton complete his turn without slowing down.

McDuffie thought it best to get out of the buffalo's way. The only problem was that the buffalo was moving faster than Chili could run. The sorrel and its well-dressed rider headed directly for the hill, the high ground of the good churchgoing folks. Surely, he will stop, murmured the congregation. We have the rope here. No one is in danger. There are rules and commandments that must be observed.

McDuffie's horse cleared the rope by yards and its hooves shattered the preacher's picnic basket when they came down. After that, general pandemonium broke loose. The rope, still intact, got caught in Cotton's horns. That rope mowed people down like a sickle until Cotton got so far past the good churchgoing folks that it snapped. The loose end recoiled around the preacher, wrapping him almost perfectly like a mummy.

Tired of the uphill climb, horse and rider made a gradual turn to the west, now on a collision course with darky hill. But those folks were not protected by the Colonel's rope and were not stupid enough to think Cotton was prepared to observe any rules, man-made or otherwise. They scattered quickly. McDuffie and Cotton passed right through them unharmed. Those mostly inebriated individuals closest to Nuncio's had the best seats in the house for both passings, if they were even aware that there was a passing.

McDuffie and Chili headed for the river. They launched themselves off a low bank and landed midstream. This seemed to pacify Cotton, who stopped as quickly as he had started and returned to his shade tree.

Not waiting for the crowd to compose themselves, the Colonel continued with the festivities. "Ladies and gentlemen, now for the last contestant, our district attorney, T. Roliff Harrington III."

The Colonel placed particular emphasis on the "III."

"And, our soon-to-be county judge," responded Harrington. With bridle in hand, he walked his black thoroughbred toward Colonel Whitworth.

"Let's take it one race at a time. Harrington, aren't you going to mount that horse?"

"My horse will be ridden by Mr. Ocy McCoy," said Harrington, gesturing at Ocy, who walked behind him. It was obvious that McCoy wasn't keen on being anywhere near Colonel Whitworth.

"That makes this a historic occasion!"

"How so, Colonel?"

"It will be the first time that there is more intelligence under the saddle than in the saddle!" The comment caused a roar of laughter from the crowd, particularly from those seated on darky hill.

McCoy glared at the Colonel, but couldn't muster a retort of any kind.

"Harrington, I guess there is no problem with McCoy riding your horse. I didn't expect a Yankee from Boston to challenge old Cotton very much."

"The War is over, Colonel. You lost—or have you forgotten?"

"Maybe so, but the Yankee Cavalry didn't win it. Anyway, get him mounted. Your ten minutes is about to start."

The last-minute substitution of McCoy did not dampen the wagering. Without a doubt, this horse would have plenty of speed, assuming McCoy could get him into position.

Harrington turned to McCoy. "Go after him quick and hard. That buffalo should be pretty winded after that last little chase."

"Yes, sir." McCoy saddled up and stared toward the tree that had now become Cotton's home base—that is, his good eye looked in that general direction. It was anyone's guess what his lazy eye was looking at.

McCoy kneed the thoroughbred into a smooth lope down toward the bottom area. Those who had never seen a thoroughbred were amazed at how much ground he covered in one stride. The quarter horses and cow ponies of Monaville could not match this animal for speed. The question was how an old winded buffalo would do.

Cotton took the bait. He left the coolness of his shade tree as McCoy approached. Then, without much provocation, Cotton charged right at the horse. McCoy was quick enough to sidestep the buffalo, but had to hold on to his saddle horn just to keep from falling off. Cotton wheeled quickly and hooked his massive head under the hindquarters of the thoroughbred. The horse may have had speed, but Cotton gave no indication that he was going to let this event turn into a race. McCoy had been busy trying to enlarge the loop on his lasso. Cotton was a good deal larger than he had guessed from a distance. Bellowing and snorting, horse and rider found themselves being driven toward a large post oak. There wasn't much they could do. The thoroughbred could get no traction and was moving his front legs as fast as he could while Cotton pushed him sideways. McCoy, at this point, was just holding on, having to raise one of his legs up over the horse's withers just to avoid getting gouged with a horn. With one last massive push, the buffalo rammed the horse and rider into the post oak with a violent thud that caused acorns to drop by the dozens. McCoy's colorful vocabulary could be heard over the horse's sounds of pain and the jingle of the stirrups now dangling completely loose.

Cotton turned slightly, giving McCoy just enough time to gather his thoughts and spur the thoroughbred to movement. Just as they were about to spring free, Cotton hit the horse's hindquarters again, only this time, the horse's legs slipped and the buffalo rolled horse and rider over.

By now, the crowd knew this was not going to be a horse race, buffalo race, or race of any sort. This was a wrestling match. McCoy was coming to the same conclusion, and rather than stay near the large angry buffalo, McCoy took off on foot. This was a huge error in judgment. There were bloodweeds in the bottom taller than McCoy. His legs were no match for Cotton's. The rattling leaves of the bloodweeds directed Cotton's attention to McCoy, who was losing ground rapidly. Dodge and weave, stumble and fall, McCoy was in full flight. The thoroughbred had left for parts unknown, and McCoy was trying to seek safety in the direction of the crowd. Only this time, the crowd had learned a lesson and was now in full retreat.

Closer and closer, buffalo and sharecropper were making their way through the rest of the bloodweed patch. The weeds ended, and a section of short, grazed grass now cushioned McCoy's footsteps. He was completely visible to the crowd and, more important, to Cotton. Without any doubt, McCoy could feel the hot breath of that old buffalo that should not have been able to run this fast for this long. Cotton lowered his head. His right horn caught McCoy's pants and with a slight flick of his head, he launched McCoy into a perfect arc. McCoy landed exactly in the middle of the cotton wagon that had heretofore been the Colonel's betting den. McCoy hit so hard that the shock knocked all the wax out of his ears and every bit of breath out of his lungs.

Colonel Whitworth leaned over McCoy, whose eyes were open but glazed and unseeing. The Colonel called for some water. Cotton had moved off and was grazing some of the short grass he had run across in his dash with McCoy. Nuncio poured a bucket of water on McCoy, who inhaled and then coughed. He blinked hard. He had to be alive. No one ever expected to die and see Colonel Whitworth when they woke up.

"Mr. McCoy, you seem to have lost your horse."

With that, Colonel Whitworth blew his horn signaling that time had expired. Cotton grazed peacefully, as participants and spectators returned to Monaville.

CHAPTER 7

Jupiter

COTTON REMAINED IN THE Oakridge river bottom. Perhaps, he enjoyed the excitement. But, then again, where was an old buffalo to go? Colonel Whitworth, knowing a moneymaker when he saw one, continued to provide the sweet feed that kept Cotton in the neighborhood. Of course, the Colonel would have to let some time lapse so that folks would forget about how he'd lined his pockets with the money they'd lost and he'd won.

Monaville chattered collectively for weeks about each and every aspect of the Great Buffalo Ropin'. However, gradually, the pattern and monotony of cotton growing returned. Afton was still ankle deep in turtles and getting deeper. It seemed that her turtles had personality, or so she thought. She was having difficulty converting her pets to soup. Old Lady Hightower was giving me more free time to do projects. Projects meant I didn't have to actually attend school. I just turned in reports. This gave me more time with my grandpa and more time with Blue. Both men were far more educational than Edwina Hightower.

I settled up with Broken Feather, who, much to my surprise, bought some new clothes with his winnings. I expected Nuncio would get the lion's share, but he didn't. I had done rather well for myself—far better than if I had actually roped that old bull. The hardest part was keeping my success a secret. I doubted that Grandpa or my parents would approve. On the Colonel's recommendation, I actually put the money in the bank. And best of all, the Colonel now called on me regularly to do chores and odd jobs when he could find no one else.

Some years ago, someone had planted sugarcane along the river on the Oakridge Plantation. It had to have been planted because no other plantation had any. More than likely, families or slaves moving into Texas brought it over from Louisiana. During the War, a lot of planters across the South relocated their slaves to Texas with hopes of keeping them, or at least keeping them from the reach of the Federals. Their assumption was that the South would win and the slaves would be returned to where they came from.

During the War, that small patch of cane had expanded. It wasn't a cash crop back then; therefore, there was no benefit in harvesting it. Cotton was still king, but there were fewer hands, black or white, to cultivate it. The planters were fighting the Yankees. Only M. E. Brown, our current sheriff, invoked the twenty-slave rule to avoid the War. Every other planter, many who owned more than twenty slaves, left Monaville to fight, some taking several slaves with them for the duration. Those folks that remained planted less. They either weren't inclined to do more or simply couldn't harvest any more. M. E Brown's plantation would have stayed in full production, except for Brown's fondness for alcohol and high living. After the War, Big Charlie figured he could make some money with the sugarcane.

The Colonel asked me to deliver a rather large cane press to Big Charlie. I had access to my grandpa's draft horses that could easily manage the load. It arrived in a large crate from Tennessee; it was heavy, rectangular in shape, with a series of rollers inside. To operate the press, you fed cut cane into one side. A metal shaft attached to a long wooden pole stuck out of the top of the press and was connected to the rollers that pressed the cane. One of Big Charlie's worn-out horses was hooked to the wooden pole and walked around the press in a circle all day. There was not much strain on the horse, but as it made its circle, the big rollers pulled in the cane and crushed it. Juice flowed out of the bottom of the press and into a big tub, and the crushed cane came out the other side. Across the front of this contraption was the word "Chattanooga," which had to be about the strangest word I'd ever seen.

Big Charlie had found that some of the older freedwomen knew how to cook the juice and make syrup. No one could say Big Charlie wasn't an enterprising soul. Colonel Whitworth agreed to buy all the syrup Charlie made, or better said, all he wanted to sell. A good bit of it disappeared during the tasting process. When Big Charlie made the delivery to the Colonel, every woman who'd had a hand in the process accompanied him. Charlie and those ladies had agreed on what everyone was going to get for their efforts. What they got wasn't cash money, but credit at the Colonel's store, which was as good as cash to them. These ladies had few belongings so whatever they wanted could most likely be found at the Colonel's store. It seemed all on the up-and-up to me. Initially, the credit concept was a little foreign to them, but they got the hang of it pretty quickly. Anyway, the participants were happy. It was the nonparticipants who had a problem. They were inclined to neither work for Big Charlie nor see anyone else get the benefit of Charlie's operation.

It didn't take much to figure out the problem. A casual ride through the river bottom explained everything. The cotton crops were as varied as the people growing them. Those croppers who knew what they were doing or were the least bit diligent could expect a pretty good return. Big Charlie was clearly out in front. He was working the same land he had always planted. He knew it and he knew how to plant it. Plus, some of the former slaves of Oakridge had, shall we say, gone on a lark, leaving more land for Charlie to plant—a good bit more than the acreage the Colonel had given him.

What was becoming profoundly obvious was that some of the croppers would soon find themselves deeper in debt to the Colonel or whoever had advanced the seed money. This alone would've caused a good bit of jealousy or hard feelings.

Charlie had inadvertently created a means for some of the freed people to have another source of income besides cotton. The great irony was that Charlie didn't and couldn't conceive of giving work to a white person—man or woman. The white croppers who were most upset would've never considered working for a Negro, period. This did not help matters, particularly for Ocy McCoy and his relatives. The McCoys were not good farmers from the get-go. The Colonel had refused to extend them any more credit; yet, credit at the Colonel's store was what the McCoys needed, and Ocy saw the sugarcane operation as the way to get it. But Ocy wasn't about to work for any former slave, and no former slave was going to get ahead of Ocy McCoy. Just how far McCoy and his night-riding Klansmen would go came as a shock to all of Monaville.

Blue's shop was strangely still. There was no breeze this morning and no sound of metal on metal or metal on stone. The large cottonwood leaves just hung on the limbs dripping dew. I rode into the stable area, but saw no sign of Blue. I heard the first heart-wrenching sob as I dismounted. It was Blue. I recognized his weeping. My first thought was to leave. It was so unusual. By this time on any other morning, Blue would have been sweat soaked and deep in his work.

I approached the back of the stable where Blue lived. I caught sight of his round form, kneeling next to one of his caskets, resting his arms on the lid. The weeping just seemed to go on and on, without any pause.

It didn't seem right to stand there and watch a grown man cry his heart out, but what could I do? I approached Blue slowly, shuffling my feet, hoping that the noise would alert him. Fortunately it did, and he turned and looked at me with bloodshot eyes.

"Blue, what is it? What has happened?"

"They kilt him, John Ross. They kilt him. He's dead."

Blue dealt with death on a routine basis. Like most colored folks, he never said "died." People passed. When I heard him say "dead," it sent a chill down my back.

"Who is dead? Who killed who?"

"Jupiter. The Kluxers kilt him, just kilt him. Dey just kilt him for no reason."

Jupiter was Big Charlie's oldest son, a good bit older than me. From what I could tell, he was the perfect image of Big Charlie as a young man. He and his father were cut from the same cloth—both were hardworking men.

"When did it happen?"

"Dey found him dis mornin' hanged to a tree, naked, and cut up."

"Have they told the sheriff?"

"Sheriff? John Ross, da sheriff ain't goin' to be no help. He's one of 'em."

"Does the Colonel know?"

"Yes, he woke me this mornin'."

"I'm sure my grandpa doesn't know. I'm going to tell him. Do you need me to do anything? Are you all right, Blue?"

"Nothin' you can do for me, John Ross. Yes, tell da General."

I spurred my Appaloosa in the direction of Catalpa, thanking heaven that my grandpa was so predictable. I knew where to find him. The moment I caught sight of him, I started hollering. He turned the bay toward me and cantered in my direction.

The news simply transformed him. He sat more erect in his saddle. His face was ashen now, almost drained of blood, but his eyes were intense and seemed fixed on some place far away.

"Where is Big Charlie now?"

"I don't know, sir. I didn't ask Blue."

"Do you know where Colonel Whitworth is?"

"No, sir, but he's the one who told Blue."

"Go find Colonel Whitworth. Tell him to meet me at the Wilhite Cemetery as soon as possible. Tell him to come alone."

"Yes, sir."

Grandpa rode off in the direction of the Catalpa bottom; no doubt he was going to tell my father the news. I headed for Colonel Whitworth's store. It was the first place I thought of, but as I rode toward Monaville, I decided to take the Oakridge road, thinking the Colonel might be there.

Things were extremely quiet. No one was around. I suspected that everyone had gathered at Big Charlie's. I thought about heading in that direction, but Grandpa wanted the Colonel to come alone, and I didn't know how to tell that to the Colonel with people around. As I reached the hillcrest overlooking the Colonel's homestead, I saw the Colonel's buggy. It didn't take much effort to catch up to a one-horse buggy hauling a 300-pound man.

"Colonel! Colonel!"

He slowed the horse and buggy. Before he had a chance to say anything, I pulled my Appy to a halt alongside him.

"Colonel, my grandpa wanted me to tell you to meet him at the Wilhite Cemetery and to come alone."

"Come alone? There isn't anyone here but me. I assume he's heard about Jupiter?"

"Yes, sir. I just told him . . . I heard when I got to Blue's this morning."

"Blue carries a heavy burden. He buries us all. It has to take its toll. Jupiter was like a son to him, since he had no children of his own."

"Yes, sir."

"If your grandpa said alone, I know he means alone. You ought to go back and stay with Blue. Some company will do him good."

"Yes, sir."

I left the Colonel as he turned his buggy around and started for the cemetery.

*   *   *

Age had pulled these two old friends in opposite directions. The General was razor thin and growing more straight and rigid each year. The Colonel was now round and corpulent. Their younger years were spent barefoot, running along the same river bottom on adjoining cotton plantations. Today, neither was personally growing cotton. The General tolerated it as a crop to be raised by sharecroppers. The Colonel financed it, but had become a city dweller, enjoying his ancestral home only as a retreat from business pressures. Today, they would meet to discuss what to do about the tragedy visited upon their mutual childhood friend, Big Charlie. The General spoke first. "Reams, what do you know about this?" Direct and right to the point, he wasted no time on pleasantries. The General knew that something had to be done. He could not and would not tolerate this kind of behavior in his hometown. As impatient as he was to move beyond slave times, some things just demanded immediate attention.

"Charlie found Jupiter down by the cane press—naked, mutilated, and tied to a tree. Jupiter always checked the fires last thing every evening when the women cooked syrup, and Charlie didn't think much about it when he didn't come home. He was a young man and, well, sometimes he kept his own hours. But Charlie had an uneasy feeling and got up before sunup to ride the bottom. The cane press was the last place he checked. Most of the problems have been around the fields with the livestock and equipment. It has gradually gone from petty theft to destruction of crops and equipment.

"Everyone knows who's doing it, Leander. But since the cane press is an old woman's operation, no one expected much of a problem."

"Reams, I don't believe it had anything to do with whose work it was. It had everything to do with who was getting ahead and who wasn't. This is a fight over who is going to stand on the bottom rung of the ladder—freed people or some of our white croppers."

"I hadn't thought of it that way, Leander, but I suspect you're right. I knew the early stuff was pretty much directed by the district attorney. My folks vote. In fact, they probably are a fair size in number and Harrington daren't risk them showing up to cast their ballots."

"As long as Brown is sheriff, ballots aren't going to mean much anyway. He counts the votes and controls the voting boxes."

"M. E. isn't his pa, that's for sure. The old man would just die if he saw his place."

"But that is the point, Reams. Sheriff Brown owes a king's ransom in taxes. He has to hitch his cart to Harrington's political future, or so he thinks."

"Leander, do you think Harrington had Jupiter killed?"

"Hard to say. Certainly not directly. Harrington wants the judgeship so he can acquire land cheaply and quickly. He'll need croppers to work it, and I doubt he cares what color they are. The problem is that some of his Kluxer friends have walked too long in the shadow of our great district attorney. They think they have power that they don't really have. We both know that their crops will fail again this year like they have before. Charlie and some others seem to be doing well, certainly far better than the Kluxers. No, the killin' had nothing to do with the election, but everything to do with where people stand. We fought one war over slavery. These bastards want to fight it over again.

"The cane press may have been the last straw. I understand the women who work the press get credit at your store. That is something some of the croppers would like to have, but don't."

"Hell, Leander, we both know who done it. Ocy McCoy and his tribe are the most desperate croppers in the bottom. Ocy couldn't even look at me at the buffalo ropin'. Of course, I suspect my comments may not have pleased him much either."

"I have no idea what you said, Reams, but I have never known you to miss an opportunity to gig someone who needed jabbing. Silence is a virtue unknown to you. Besides McCoy, Brown, and Harrington, who else is a party, or better said, how many other Kluxers do we have?"

"McCoy has three cousins in the bottom. One has a son who rides with them, so that would make seven plus a cropper named Jed Terry. There could be more, but I've seen those in close conversations in town."

"Croppers in town—that helps explain why their crops are so poor."

"You got to do what you do best. Apparently, creating trouble is their strong suit. Do you have a plan, Leander?"

"Where do they meet? When we have had problems, we've been able to track most of the Kluxers back to the old abandoned Baptist church—you know, back in the woods, not far from Brown's plantation."

"Yes, I know the place. I want to make sure we have them all when we make our move. Tell Charlie I'm working on something, but tell him to hold his anger, Reams. There will be a time. Meanwhile, you need to be careful. It's credit at your store that they all need, so right now you are a very large obstacle."

"You aren't referring to my weight?"

"Not directly, but you do make an easy target. I suggest you stay near town. If you're coming out to Oakridge, have someone come with you. You are way too exposed out here. Do you know when Charlie will have the funeral?"

"No, not yet, but I'll send word," said the Colonel.

"These folks are dangerous, Reams. They think they are above the law. In many ways, they are. We have an alcoholic sheriff tied to a Yankee DA who has political ambitions. You and I are disenfranchised. I'm fearful that we have one more campaign in front of us. I thought . . . no, I had hoped that my battle plans were all behind me. Let me follow you to the edge of town. Then I have some work to do."

The old friends parted within sight of Monaville. The death of Jupiter weighed heavy on the Colonel's mind. He'd had good intentions when he'd divided the lands around Oakridge among its slaves. Yes, he'd had something to gain as the town's leading merchant. But in his heart, it had felt like the right thing to do. The cane press was progress. Big Charlie was making a go of it. True enough, some of his people had failed or were likely to fail soon, but the Oakridge freedmen made about as much money as the white sharecroppers. Whitworth never anticipated the petty jealousies among so many people. The General was probably right. There were no slaves anymore. Someone had to stand on the bottom rung. It hurt him that his good intentions had brought about the death of the son of one of his best friends. The General got that much right.

What he had missed was how the district attorney was tied to all the violence. Leander hadn't come to town more than a couple of times since the War ended. He wasn't aware of how often McCoy and his tribe were seen with the DA, and as for the sheriff, well, the jail was nothing more than a hangout for the McCoy clan. As the Colonel reflected on it, there was more of a pattern to the mischief than appeared at first glance.

Monaville's old elite were all disenfranchised. Unreconstructed Rebels couldn't vote, become jurors, or hold office. The Freedmen's Bureau had never really opened up shop in this area. They couldn't even get a foothold in East Texas, much less the Brazos Valley. It seemed that their officers in charge showed up dead far too often. As a result, Monaville's behavior was pretty much in the hands of T. Roliff Harrington III and a handful of white voters. Whenever a jury was needed, some all-too-convenient mischief happened that encouraged black jurors to find cause to stay home. The pattern seemed obvious when you charted the Klan's mischief against its need to ensure that the newly franchised freedmen did not exercise their franchise.

Mentally, the Colonel retraced the actions of the Kluxers. Their footsteps were leading directly to the doorstep of Monaville's most prominent Yankee—Mr. Harrington.

*   *   *

The morning fog drifted around the cottonwoods. It was past sunup, but you could hardly tell. Blue raised himself up from his bed. He was emotionally exhausted—far more fatigued from grief than he'd ever been from physical labor. He gradually moved toward the back of the barn, which was totally enveloped in the foggy mist. Glancing toward the front of the barn, he found he could see no better in that direction.

His eyes caught some movement near the cottonwoods, or maybe it was just swirling fog. For whatever reason, Blue was drawn to it. He stepped outside, but still saw nothing. He took one more step and thought he must be dreaming. A figure was there, so familiar, but from so long ago, standing so still, so quiet.

It took a moment. The fog clouded his vision and the years clouded his mind. Then it came to him like a shot.

"General, dat you?"

"Yes. I hope I didn't startle you, Blue."

"No, sir, I seen you like dat many times. Quiet as a church mouse."

"Blue, take this list. Do you recognize the names?"

"Yes, sir. I know dese men."

"Do you shoe their horses?"

"Yes, sir."

"Can you mark their shoes so I can track them?"

"Preddy sure I can."

"How long will it be before all their horses will be shod?"

"Mr. Harrington was in last . . . so a month at da most."

"Fine. I'll check with you. Needless to say, this will just be between you and me."

"Just likes it always been."

"I appreciate that, Blue. I'm not going to let them get away with killing Jupiter—you know that, don't you?"

"Yes, sir. I knowed you wud do somethin'."

"What about that other project, are they ready?"

"Yes, sir, but I hope it's a long time 'fore dey's needed."

"Blue, it seems things are getting more violent and more uncertain every day. Safeguard them. You know what I want."

"Yes, sir."

The General and his bay horse disappeared into the fog, and Blue had his marching orders once again.

CHAPTER 8

Growin' Up Is Serious Business

HE COULDN'T HAVE BEEN gone more than a day at the most. Grandpa rode the pastures methodically. He might miss a cow one day but would be certain to look for and find her the next. Now a bull, that was a little different. He once had a big black bull named Romeo. You never saw him in the daylight. When I say never, I mean never, because Grandpa and my pa both sent me looking for him on many occasions. Looking for a black bull in the Texas sun isn't fun. Lying up under some tree, they just can't be seen. I would crisscross pastures and look for gaps in fences, coming close to exhausting my horse and myself. At sundown, I could hear him bellow and blow. That's when I knew he was still around. For an invisible bull, he produced some of the best calves we ever had.

However, I don't think Grandpa could handle the uncertainty of never being able to see him. After Romeo, he didn't buy any more black bulls. He wanted some white on them somewhere so he could find them. Nothing against black bulls, Grandpa just wanted to be able to count critters as he drifted through a pasture. And, he wanted the count to tally every day. Grandpa liked certainty.

Grandpa and I had spent all day moving cattle. I was tired. He had to be, but I don't remember him showing it. At least he never admitted he was tired. We rode into the barn together. I unsaddled the horses and took care of the tack. I suspect this chore had been done for him during the War by some private, but there were no more privates, and I was around and was glad to do it. I always wanted to hear more about the War, the battles, the armaments. Lord knows I hinted enough, but Grandpa never spoke of the War. I could piece some things together based on what I overheard from others. Grandpa was a cavalry officer. There were not many engagements in the East that he missed. The Monaville men seemed to credit him with getting them home, mostly in one piece. Being his grandson opened doors for me in a sense, but there was always a quiet distance between him and the average citizens of Monaville that was hard to describe. A confused mixture of respect, fear, and mystery would be the most accurate summation. One thing was certain, among the men that rode off to the War with him, there was total loyalty to my grandpa. I guess this made me loyal as well.

I could remove the tack, feed the horses, and take care of the saddles. Grandpa brushed the big bay. I don't know if he liked doing it or if he felt he ought to as a payback. For whatever reason, I wasn't the one to brush that horse. He and Grandpa had some kind of bond that only another horse lover would understand. He and that bay were a unit. Even after he lost his leg, Grandpa never had to spur his horse. That bay knew where he was to go and at what pace. They were of one mind and that mind was Grandpa's.

My father usually arrived at the barn about the same time as Grandpa and me. I always listened intently to their conversations.

Sometimes the noise of my chores or the horses would drown out parts of their talk. If I got too quiet, they knew I was listening and would sometimes cut things short. I had to adopt a middle-of-the-road approach. I kept to my chores, but tried to go about them as quietly as I could.

For the most part, they talked about the daily routine of the plantation. Crops, weather, cattle, and horses were always mentioned in their daily banter. However, as the growing season progressed, the sharecroppers became a main focus. By now, my pa could predict who was going to make it and who would fall deeper into debt. If it was so obvious to my pa, I wondered, why wouldn't the croppers know it themselves? Perhaps some did. Others survived on hope. The weather this year had worked in everyone's favor. I hated to think how poor some of the folks were. The Weibergs were good, hardworking people. Their survival hinged on a single harvest of a single crop. I hoped that I could build a place for myself on the plantation among Grandpa's cattle or horses. Sharecropper operations just depressed me.

After Jupiter's death, their conversations became more interesting, but Pa and Grandpa seemed more guarded in what they said. Any indication that I was listening and they were likely to finish their discussion outside the barn. This left me frustrated and alone with my chores. This much I could gather—Grandpa was more than a little upset, not just with the killing, but also with the lack of any form of justice to avenge the murder. On one hand, he wanted to avenge the death, while on the other hand, he resented the fact that the responsibility for action fell on him at this time in his life. What he had planned, I didn't know, but I could rest assured that his cavalry company from Monaville would be involved. For several weeks they covered the daily routine topics and then automatically moved outside, always much to my disappointment.

One evening they were already outside, and I was trimming the Appy's hooves. I noticed that things had gotten rather quiet—still, would be a better word.

I was bent over alongside the horse when I looked up. Standing shoulder-to-shoulder down at the south end of this northbound horse stood my pa and grandpa, both looking at me. They weren't talking. There was no clear expression on their faces, or none that I could read, anyway. I quickly reviewed my activities of the not-too-distant past. I had no recollection of any personal misconduct on my part that would justify the need to assemble two generations of Wilhites. I was at a loss. Why would both of them be standing there looking at me? Their similarity in appearance was more stark and noticeable to me than ever before. Sizewise, they were identical. The only real difference was that my father had wavy black hair whereas Grandpa's was straight and gray. I couldn't recall ever seeing them standing so close to each other. But here they were. What did it mean?

My pa spoke first. "John Ross, may we have a word with you? That Appy can hold a minute or two, don't you think?"

"Yes, sir," my voice cracking just enough to remind me that I still had some growin' to do.

"Why don't we take a seat over on those barrels? My leg doesn't feel like holding me up much longer. I think it needs a rest."

Grandpa's suggestion was welcome. I wasn't sure that I might not just fall over myself from nerves.

The barrels had been here as long as I had. I suppose they once had a real purpose, but for as long as I could remember, they were furniture—barn furniture. We sat on them. My grandpa moved his barrel. He now sat directly in front of me. I glanced at my pa, who smiled quietly. I suspected he had been on this same barrel, positioned in front of Grandpa, once or twice before. This was little comfort to me now.

"John Ross, it appears you have pretty much completed your schoolwork with Miss Hightower."

"Yes, sir, I suspect so."

"What are your plans, son?"

Now this was a bolt out of the blue. What were my plans! Well, what were they? I hadn't given it, or them, any thought. Now, the General was asking me what my plans were.

"Sir, I'm not sure what you mean."

"Fair enough. Do you see yourself making Monaville your home—either here at Catalpa or elsewhere?"

While I appreciated the explanation, I saw Monaville and Catalpa as one unless Grandpa was contemplating my eviction. The thought left me rudderless.

"Sir, I have always hoped that I could continue to live here . . . at Catalpa."

"Is that important to you, John Ross?"

"Yes, sir."

"Why?"

Good God, the General had a basketful of questions. I knew this was serious business. This wasn't going to be just a sit-on-Grandpa's-lap-and-tell-stories moment.

"It is my home, sir. I was born here and have never thought about leaving Catalpa. It is the home of my parents, your home, and the home of your parents. I guess it is where Wilhites are supposed to be."

"Would you die for it, son?"

"Die for it . . . I have never thought about that. I do love it, every square foot of it. I suppose I would."

"I rode off to the War with young men your age, some even younger. That horrific conflict made a lot of boys into men very quickly, John Ross. Folks will tell you what caused that War. In truth, every man who participated probably had his own reasons for getting involved in it. However, for the most part, it was a reaction. I never met anyone in any of the armies of the South who went looking for that fight. It was nothing more than the same reaction anyone would have, you included, when they feel that their way of life is threatened."

"Yes, sir." I was starting to wonder if I had missed the coming of another war. Grandpa's body leaned toward me, making the interrogation all the more intense. I cast a quick glance down at his peg leg. If we were discussing war, I knew it was serious.

"When I returned, I thought I was through with the fightin'. I just wanted to get to work and put everything related to the War behind me. It now appears that I . . . I should say we—me, your pa, and you—have a fight on our hands."

"We do?"

"Yes, we do, John Ross. If you intend to make Catalpa your home, and I heard you say that you do, then you are going to have to join the fight. The future belongs to you, son . . . you and your pa. If Catalpa is going to remain a place fit to live—where you would want to live—then we must take control of some things now."

"You know that neither your pa, nor I, nor any of us who fought for the South can vote."

"Yes, sir."

"We can't hold office. We can't do much of anything to lead Monaville into the future. The power and control rests with folks who have little character, who care less than nothing about this community, and who want to line their own pockets.

"You know that Big Charlie's son Jupiter was murdered."

"Yes, sir."

"Do you know who did it?"

"No, sir."

"No idea, John Ross?"

"Well, I have heard talk about the Kluxers."

"Do you know why they did it?"

"No, sir."

"They did it because they could. They are thoroughly convinced that they are above the law, that they will not be challenged, and that they will be in control of Monaville in the near future. Does that sound like the place you want to live?"

"No, sir!"

"Your pa and I have talked a great bit about whether we should get you involved at all. You are just a young man. If your mother knew we were having this talk, she would raise unmitigated hell. But every man I saw killed during the War was some mother's baby. Sooner or later, we all have to quit being some mother's baby and start being a man, to protect our homes and our families so that others will have a chance to be some mother's baby, at least for a while. Plus, we need your help."

"You do?"

"Yes, son, we do."

"Whether you know it or not, you are a fixture on the landscape. People have seen you moving around this county for years. It's what you do. No one gives it a second thought. You are the exact opposite of me. I seldom leave the plantation. Lately it seems I leave Catalpa for funerals and nothing else."

He seemed to drift a little, taking a long pause as if he was reflecting on recent burials.

"Your pa and I, with the help of a very select few, are going to take our community back. I need you to be my eyes."

I looked up to find Grandpa staring deep into my eyes, almost into my heart and soul. I have never seen him look at me with such total concentration.

"You are familiar with the old abandoned Baptist church?"

"Yes, sir, I am."

"How many ways can you get there?"

"The two roads are the most obvious, but there are at least a half dozen pig trails in and around the area. I know them all. And, if you want to take the river, there's a creek that you can use to get within shouting distance."

"I had totally forgotten about the creek. John Ross, I want you to choose a couple of geldings from the remuda. Make them solid brown or chestnut. Be sure they are of a quiet nature and that you can ground tie them. Leave the Appaloosa here at Catalpa. Keep him close to the house. If anyone asks why you're not riding him, tell them you're mending a hoof.

"You are now a scout. Scouts don't ride Appys. That spotted blanket of his draws too much attention even in the brush. I want you to keep an eye on that church, but stay off the roads. You stay in the brush. When you get within a couple hundred yards of the church, ground tie your horse and move away from him. Don't tie him to any tree or bush. A lot of scouts have been killed because their horses were shaking a tree limb. You get away from him while you're observing the church. Put an old skiff near that creek. If your horse leaves or gets seen, you leave by way of the river. You just float home, you hear?"

"Yes, sir."

"Never approach that church from the same way twice in a row. I'll give you my field glasses to use. Keep them out here in the barn. I don't want your mother to get suspicious. Report to me whenever you see anyone and tell me who's in the party. You are not to discuss this with anyone, ever. And I mean it should remain your life's secret. Do you understand?"

"Yes, sir."

"Now we had better get inside. The womenfolk will be wondering what we are up to, no doubt."

Grandpa rose and placed his hand on my shoulder. I looked up at him. He smiled slightly and said, "You'll do fine, John Ross."

That night I heard no sounds coming from his room, so I knew he was sleeping as soundly as he ever had. I certainly didn't.

CHAPTER 9

Momma Mae

IT TOOK VERY LITTLE imagination on my part to enlarge my scouting duties into something far greater than they actually were. Soon I was riding with that great cavalry officer, General Leander Wilhite, outside of Chancellorsville, or was it Gettysburg? All the places that I knew he had been, and never spoke of, flashed vividly through my imagination. However, reality had a way of injecting a certain dullness into my pretend games.

I did my homework and soon knew every pig trail in, around, and to the old church. I selected my horses. I even tested them one Sunday on my own church congregation. I convinced my parents, well, at least my mother, that I wasn't feeling too good. She wasn't even out of sight before I was astride a brown gelding. Trailing a set of parents in a carriage with twin redheads wasn't that much of a challenge, as I'm sure my sisters commandeered all the attention my parents could spare. The twins had an extraordinary curiosity about me, and on more than one occasion, their unwanted attention had caused me some pain. I trailed their carriage to and fro and circumnavigated the entire congregation without incident.

The old Baptist church was not used during the day. After many long and boring waits, it became obvious that it functioned as a meeting place only after dark. A small number of Kluxers would gather on Friday evenings, with a larger number present on Saturday evenings. Mr. Harrington only participated on Saturday. Friday was left pretty much to the McCoys and their friends.

Since my grandpa and father knew of my project, getting out of the house only required me to offer some satisfactory reason to my mother. This was when I learned to truly appreciate the value of my sisters. By the end of the day, my mother wanted only one thing—peace. If I had told her that I was leaving to rob the Monaville Bank, I think she would have said, "Fine, now just be careful." Grandpa and Pa came up with quite an assortment of excuses that kept me in the saddle. Once I figured out the Klansmen's established pattern, things became easier.

I had started to develop a little confidence in my scouting abilities. I hadn't quite convinced myself that I was invisible, but I could move through the thicket around that old church pretty well. I had been out late one Saturday night. It was a full-moon evening. Folks referred to it as a Comanche Moon. The countryside was almost as clear as in daylight once your eyes adjusted. You had to be particularly careful because every predator in the animal world was moving about. Comanches were just about the only creatures not moving around, thanks to my Wilhite ancestors.

I returned to the horse barn generally pleased with myself. To reduce the chance of waking my mother, I simply unsaddled the horse and stabled him. Cleaning him up could wait until morning.

As I crossed the barnyard headed toward the house, I heard a creak. It was both an unmistakable sound and a familiar one. It was Momma Mae's rocker. The roofline of her quarters extended out a ways past the stone wall of the kitchen. Her rocker rested on a wooden-plank porch. If you didn't know to look for her, you wouldn't have seen her. She placed her rocker in the darkest corner of the porch. Anyone raised on Catalpa knew that sound. We had all been lulled to sleep way too many times by Momma Mae, her humming, and the creak of her rocker. No use fighting it, I headed in her direction. I stepped up on the porch. She was dipping snuff and seemed to be enjoying it.

"You out pretty late."

"Yes, ma'am."

"John Ross, now you not gonna tell an old woman all those stories your pa and grandpa has been tellin' your momma, are you? Momma Mae been here a long time. I sees a whole lot from dis porch. Could see more when da quarters were dere. But I still sees a lot."

I wasn't sure where she was going, but I knew she could quickly get at the truth if she wanted to.

"Yes, ma'am."

"You been comin' and goin' a lot late at night. But I knowed your grandpa and pa knows what you're doin'. Has to. Tellin' your momma you checkin' calves, huh? You got all your calves on da ground. So all you men are up to somethin'."

"Momma Mae, I can't tell you." It took all the courage I could muster to say that. I didn't dare stand there and answer questions because without a doubt she would or could get to where she wanted to go.

"I knowed you can't. Lord, how I knowed it. I have been here forever. I was here when da General drew his first breath. Same with your pa. Lately, dere's been a big weight on your grandpa's shoulders. Dat started when Charlie's son was kilt. I knowed it eats at him. I can feel it. I seen it before. Your grandpa feels things. You can count on him to do something. He ain't gonna forget it. I knowed it."

"You know him well, Momma Mae."

"Like the back of dis old hand. I knowed he won't stand still, but I does worry 'bout him."

"I'm not sure I've ever heard anyone say that they worried about him. I mean, he's the General."

"Ain't always been da General, son. But he has always known right from wrong. Dat's what's I worry 'bout. Men dat stand for right scare most folks. I seen dat weight on his shoulders before. He ain't gonna let it go on too far. No, not too far."

"You believe he's in danger?"

"Oh, yes, he stays here right at Catalpa most times. But any fool in Monaville gots to know he knows what's happened. For sure, dey do. Ifin you been here any time at all, you know he's comin'. Gots to scare some folks.

"Dey really scare of demselves, you know, and how dey treat people, dat includes how dey treated da General."

I was taken aback by this. It had never occurred to me how anyone treated my grandpa. He was an adult, a grown-up. I figured no one much cared or gave it any thought. Adults just pretty much went about their business. It seemed all the fightin' and arguing got taken care of and out of their systems by now, or so I thought. I was growing to appreciate that when grown-ups had disagreements, the consequences seemed more violent, certainly more severe than the typical swollen lip. But how could Grandpa be mistreated? He seldom left Catalpa.

"Momma Mae, who has ever mistreated my grandpa?"

"Who?"

"Yes, ma'am."

"All dem town folks . . . yes, all dem town folks. Da man has been a prisoner on his own plantation mosta his life."

"I thought he just wanted to stay here. He's always so busy."

"Da man knows where he's wanted . . . your grandpa ain't no fool . . ."

"But he is so intense about Monaville . . . wanted to know if I planned to stay . . ."

"Uh, he may not be wanted, but, he knows he's needed. Dis is his home. His people are buried here. Take a lot more dan some town folks to move him, yes, sir. Ain't no town folks gonna move da General, no, sir."

I was trying to make sense of all this when she continued.

"John Ross, your grandpa watches you like a hawk. Always has. Even 'fore da War. He knows we ain't here forever. He wants to make sure you becomes a man . . . a man like him. You listen to him."

"Oh, Momma Mae, I do. I wished he would talk more. He's better than school."

"No doubt 'bout dat. No, sir. He talked more as a boy."

"He did?"

"Could not hush 'em. I mean, could not hush 'em. Sometimes peoples take things out of other folks. Think da General had a lot taken out of him 'long da way. Seemed to gather more problems than his share . . . his and other folks'. Never seen him shirk, never shirk, not da General.

"John Ross, it's late. I don't know what da General has you doin'. If he wanted me to know, he would have told me. Dis I do know. All dose men dat came back wif 'em after da War, dey all say he got dem home. Whatever he has you doin', you listen to him. You do what he says and da way he wants it . . . den you'll be fine. Now you better run along."

"Yes, ma'am."

I took my boots off at the back door and cast a glance back at Momma Mae. She smiled. She knew what and why about everything that I was doing and, I suspected, about everyone else for that matter. As I slipped under the covers, I started to see that there might be more to my grandpa than I had observed. General Leander Wilhite—a talker? Impossible.

The next morning, the General and I saddled up and headed toward the Brazos River bottom. We had been riding for about fifteen minutes when I gathered all the courage my curiosity could muster and asked my grandpa the question that seemed frozen in my mind.

"Grandpa, did you used to be a talker?"

His bay horse came to a quick halt, but I didn't see him give the bay the slightest cue. There was no tug on the reins. Perhaps the bay was so shocked by my inquiry, he couldn't believe it. My grandpa turned the bay so the horse's head was facing my elbow with Grandpa right behind it. Then, my grandpa did something so unusual, it almost scared me—he grinned. Not just a big smile, but a huge grin showing me teeth that I cannot ever recall seeing before.

"John Ross, you have been talking to Momma Mae, haven't you?"

"Well, yes, sir."

There was a pause, which gave my grandpa time to chuckle and me time to collect my thoughts. But there was no further response coming.

"Sir, were you?"

"If Momma Mae says so, then, I guess I was. Lord knows, she would know."

"What happened, Grandpa? You hardly talk much at all now."

"Son, my father died before I had a chance to learn everything I needed to know about running Catalpa. It made me grow up too quickly, I suppose. I was so overwhelmed with the problems and demands, the last thing I wanted to do was to show people my inexperience. There are those people, even here in Monaville, who would take advantage of you. I decided I needed to spend more time thinking than talking, so I guess I broke myself of the habit."

"Momma Mae spoke of you having a lot of weight on your shoulders."

"I don't know that I had any more responsibilities or hardships than anyone else. Life is a challenge. You can't run from problems. You must deal with the hand that you're dealt. As the years run together, the problems tend to link up like a chain. It does change you . . . no question, things do change you. John Ross, I don't believe I have thought of those early years in a coon's age; yet, they do seem to be always with me. We have a task at hand that we must complete. Maybe when we get through with it, I could recapture some of my youth. All work and no play is supposed to make you a pretty dull person. Colonel Whitworth has reminded me of that frequently. We'll see, John Ross, we shall see."

Things appeared, just for a moment, a little brighter and maybe even lighter for my grandpa. However, as we approached the old church, his serious nature returned. We stopped in a greenbriar thicket about 200 yards from the church. He wanted to know about everything I'd seen over the past weeks. Who came from what direction? Did they come alone or in a group? Did they always follow this or that pattern? Was there any exception to the rule? He pretty much turned the whole affair over and looked at it every which way. I now appreciated why the men of Monaville returned in one piece. The General was hell on preparation.

CHAPTER 10

Ocy McCoy

COLONEL WHITWORTH'S COTTON GIN was just starting on the first bit of this year's crop. Big Charlie got his cotton planted early, as he customarily did. His crop looked good on the land he owned, not as good on some of the land he leased. Different parcels had been brought into his operation at various times. If he could keep working it, all the land he planted would gradually reach the quality of his own land. Charlie could grow anything and wasn't afraid to take on the poorest piece of dirt.

For most of the croppers, harvest began a time of hard, back-breaking work. It also was a time of excitement. Their individual and collective hope was to cover their crop loans and maybe, just maybe, reduce what they owed at Colonel Whitworth's. This annual budding of hope had frequently withered with disappointment. If there was going to be a good yield, this year's crop seemed more likely than most.

For the Kluxers, it was a time of panic. Most did not take the Colonel at his word when he said he wasn't going to gin their cotton.

In their minds, the death of one young darky shouldn't much matter. Plus, cotton was a cash crop for the grower and the ginner. But they misjudged the Colonel. Big Charlie was woven into the fabric of Monaville. These Kluxers were a transitory collection of misfits and Colonel Whitworth didn't need their cotton, their business, or their kind.

The next closest gin was a good two-day wagon ride from Monaville. Even if the Kluxers could secure the use of a wagon, or wagons, they would be spending days in useless travel and might not be able to get their entire crop to market. Travel alone increased the likelihood that they would run into one of Texas's pop-up thunderstorms. Wet cotton wouldn't sell, here or anywhere else.

As reality began to set in for Harrington's night riders, Nuncio's became the scene of more and more fights. As long as they had credit or could finagle a drink from some source, the Kluxers would gather to discuss and cuss—mostly the latter—their current predicament. As time passed, their options got narrower and narrower. They weren't about to own up to killing Jupiter. Even their friend, the district attorney, wouldn't be able to protect them from a lynch mob, which was always a possibility during these times. Even trying to move some of their cotton out of Monaville was just too much effort. Cussing was easier.

With each passing day, the line of wagons grew longer outside the Colonel's gin. The dirt streets of Monaville were quickly becoming covered with a fine powder because of the passage of so many wagons. The line could now be seen from Nuncio's. Tempers were growing short. The Colonel had the only gin in town and nothing was changing that anytime soon.

The great thing about the General's decision to get out of the cotton business was that there was no cotton to pick. Better said, no Wilhite was picking cotton. To be sure, my father was putting in some long hours making sure the sharecroppers were serious about their efforts. Most were fairly conscientious. Those who weren't wouldn't be here next year. My father had grown very weary of tending croppers. From now on, he planned to choose them with a good deal of care. A bad, lazy, or troublesome cropper did more harm than good. They were not worth the effort.

After Momma Mae's Sunday dinner, which no one in their right mind would miss, I headed into town to visit with Blue. With all of my scouting, I had almost worn out the shoes on one of the brown geldings. There was always the possibility that I might run into Afton. Having completed Edwina Hightower's best attempt at turning me into an educated person, I now only saw Afton at church. Her mother insisted on parking her right next to her on the front row. This was far too close to the preacher for my taste. I would have preferred the back row. My family's habit was to sit about five rows from the rear. This practice started when the twins were younger. My mother wanted to be in the middle of the congregation; however, when one of the little hellions cried or started a disturbance, she liked to be close enough to the exit for a quick trip outdoors. My great fear has been that Mom would move us closer to the front now that the twins could manage to sit through a service. If we moved forward, I would probably just move out of town.

Sunlight filtered through every crack and knothole opening in Blue's barn, highlighting flies, gnats, and dust particles floating in the interior of the old building. Blue had the forge going and was shoeing one of the stabled horses.

"Howdy, Blue."

"Hi, John Ross." He never missed a beat. Nails were being set just so to hold that horseshoe in place through mud, sand, water, rocky roads, or whatever terrain the horse and rider encountered. I tied my horse and started removing the old shoes.

"Looks like you waited some time to get dat horse new shoes."

I had expected a question about where the Appaloosa was. I was glad we didn't have to go down that trail.

"Oh, I've been covering some ground. Do you have time to shoe 'em?"

"Sure, got nothin' but time. John Ross, Colonel Whitworth comin' to take a ride in his buggy. Could you check da harness for me? I wants it right and I done it in a hurry."

Blue had harnessed those same horses to the same buggy for years. On a good day, he could do it in his sleep. But, I had noticed that Blue was starting to have good days and not so good days. I suspected he just wanted my reassurance.

Like a gust of wind, Colonel Whitworth and Mrs. Whitworth blew into the barn. Mrs. Whitworth was a very proper lady and carried herself as such, that is, when she wasn't following the Colonel. When accompanying the Colonel, well, he just kept her in a trot. The Colonel could cover a lot of ground very quickly—despite his girth. Mrs. Whitworth just barely kept up with his pace.

"Well, what a magnificent surprise, young Master Wilhite is here."

The Colonel had started this irritating habit of calling me young Master Wilhite since I had finished school.

"Hello, Colonel. How are you, Mrs. Whitworth?"

The Colonel gave his wife absolutely no chance to respond, but continued without interruption.

"Going to take the little woman out for a ride. Please don't tell your grandpa. He doesn't think it's safe. Actually, he doesn't think living is safe. However, we are going to risk it. Need to seize the opportunity, Master Wilhite. Yes, seize the opportunity."

While focused on the Colonel and doing what I could to make sense out of his latest pontifications, I'd failed to notice the slight figure that had entered the barn. Mrs. Whitworth had gotten seated in the buggy. Colonel Whitworth was slightly stooped with the reins in his left hand. He stepped up, finished his turn, and sat down in the buggy, taking the overwhelming majority of the bench seat. Colonel Whitworth's head turned quickly toward the figure standing in the shadow of a stall.

"Mr. McCoy, has Nuncio's burnt down?"

Blue and I turned at the same time—Blue was looking across the team of horses hitched to the buggy, while I was positioned toward the rear of the buggy.

Ocy McCoy looked totally emaciated, which was understandable given his recent diet of Nuncio's alcohol. He did not speak, but was focused exclusively on Colonel Whitworth. Although it was always hard to tell where Ocy was looking because his lazy eye tended to throw you off. However, the one badly bloodshot, straight-ahead eye was looking directly at the Colonel.

In his belt was a bowie knife, an Arkansas toothpick large enough to poke a good-sized hole in a 300-pound man. In a fluid, single motion, Ocy McCoy pulled the knife and leapt toward the Colonel. Cold, naked fear sliced right through my entire body. The Colonel did not have the reflexes of his youth, but he had sized up the situation long before either Blue or I had the slightest notion of McCoy's intent. His free right hand moved toward his vest pocket. His thumb raised the derringer up to his palm. Now armed, his right hand moved to meet McCoy's challenge. The Colonel fired just one shot from the double-barreled derringer. The bullet caught

McCoy in midflight, dropping him to the dirt-and-hay-covered floor of Blue's barn.

"God dammit, the bastard went and made me shoot him right in front of the missus."

I glanced at Mrs. Whitworth, who appeared totally dumbfounded. She sat completely still in the buggy. She held her gloved hand over her mouth, but said nothing. Blue, on the other hand, couldn't quit rubbing his face with his huge hands and muttering, "Oh Lord, oh Lord."

The Colonel stepped down from the buggy. McCoy lay facedown, obviously dead, headed for parts unknown. The shot had been loud enough to draw a few onlookers into the stable, which was now strangely still and quiet. Quiet except for Blue.

"Oh Lord, oh Lord."

"I don't know what you're 'oh Lord'ing about, Blue. This is the most convenient piece of business you will ever see. You generally have to go out and pick up your coffin customers. Well, don't you?"

"Oh Lord."

The Colonel wasn't making much headway with Blue. He turned to me and said, "John Ross, see if you can get Blue's attention long enough to find a pine box for Mr. McCoy."

"Oh Lord."

"Come on, Blue. I'll help you sort through them. It doesn't look like he'll need a very big one."

"Oh Lord, oh Lord."

Someone must have gone for the sheriff because M. E. Brown entered the stable just about that time. It was anyone's guess how long he had been drinking. Actually I don't believe he ever stopped, just slowed down at different intervals during the day. Sheriff Brown looked more than a little perplexed. In all likelihood, he came more out of instinct or curiosity than any nagging sense of duty. This had to be his first killin' in town. Monaville didn't have any killings during the War. All the men were away, except Brown. He had invoked the twenty-slave rule and stayed home. Thus, he became sheriff. No one else was around. Women couldn't be sheriff and probably had little interest anyway.

Sheriff Brown finally managed to focus on the lifeless form that had once been Ocy McCoy. While his eyes were working, he looked around the stable area. There were only five of us there. Actually, four, if you didn't count McCoy. Brown certainly wasn't going to speak to Blue, a Negro. Mrs. Whitworth would never speak to Brown, even if he wasn't a drunk. That left the Colonel and me. Since the Colonel stood closest to the body, I suppose Brown figured he should address his questions to him.

"Colonel, what happened here?" Sheriff Brown tried to put as much authority in his voice as he could given his current state of inebriation. Colonel Whitworth turned slightly.

"Jesus, Brown, are you that dense? The silly bastard is lying there straight out with a bowie knife pointed in the direction of my buggy and my wife. Can't you figure it out?"

This rocked the sheriff back on his heels, literally. He teetered there, knowing that he'd been insulted but not knowing the official response a sheriff should make, other good citizens began to gather in Blue's barn. The audience didn't need any time to figure out the crime scene. Sheriff Brown had to do something, but what, he wasn't sure. Then, in a not-so-loud voice he said, "Colonel, I must arrest you for the murder of Ocy McCoy."

"Murder, my ass! That bastard came at me with that rather large, sharp piece of steel, which is still in his hand. His obvious intent was to make my wife a widow. I acted in self-defense. McCoy may be a friend of yours and Mr. Harrington's, but he doesn't or didn't have any right to hasten my trip to the promised land. You aren't going to arrest me or anybody. I've lived here all my life. I'm not going anywhere and you know where to find me.

"John Ross, unhitch the team. I'd better forget about the ride and get Mrs. Whitworth home."

They departed through the crowd. The sheriff, still befuddled, turned to me. "Have Blue put him in a box. I guess his family will come for him."

No investigation. No questions. Sheriff Brown didn't even take the knife. For my first experience at being a witness to a crime, it all seemed rather uneventful. Uneventful for now, anyway.

*   *   *

I enjoyed my newfound but short-lived experience as a celebrity. The whole family wanted to know every detail. My mother interrupted me, expressing her concern that the discussion wasn't suitable for the dinner table. But then, she would immediately follow with a question, which renewed everyone's interest in the demise of Ocy McCoy. As was his custom, Grandpa headed upstairs shortly after dinner. I followed not too long behind him. As I passed his door, he called to me.

"John Ross, we haven't heard or seen the end of this McCoy matter. I don't know what his family will do, or for that matter, Brown or Harrington. I have a suspicion. In the meantime, I will accompany you on your scouting trips. In fact, tomorrow evening might be a good time to see if that old Baptist church will draw a crowd. I'll tell your father. Keep your wits about you, son. Good night."

My grandpa sure could take the edge off of a good night's sleep. I turned the events over in my head as many ways as I could. I was sure the General knew what to expect, but I certainly didn't.

CHAPTER 11

The Indictment

THE NEXT DAY, GRANDPA kept me real close at hand. Any chance of visiting Monaville and entertaining masses of citizens with my rendition of the facts was eliminated by the good General. We traveled our usual route. Visiting the heifer herd was the first order of business. If there were going to be any catastrophes, it would undoubtedly involve the heifers. The heifers' maternal instincts were quite amazing—having never had a calf, they somehow figured out how to lick one off, eat the afterbirth, and get the newborn up and nursing within about twenty minutes. That being said, the rest of their day was just some silly ass accident looking for a place to happen. Today was one of the few uneventful days.

Grandpa had divided the herd of mature cows into three groups. Each group had its own bull battery. Bulls stayed with their herd and, supposedly, were not to breed cows from another. That was the General's theory. However, a bull can smell a cow in season from a great distance. Therefore, we tried to position the herds so that they were not in adjoining pastures. Of course, when we moved one group, this forced us to move all of them, usually in a certain sequence.

In the early afternoon, as we were leaving the river bottom pasture along the Oakridge land, we caught sight of the Colonel's buggy. I had wondered if he was going to pay Grandpa a visit. However, the buggy wasn't going the usual speed for the Colonel, which was as fast as he could go. As it drew closer, we could see that the Colonel wasn't the driver. It was Mrs. Whitworth.

"Grandpa, that's the Colonel's buggy, but he's not driving it!"

"Who is, John Ross?" Grandpa's eyes could no longer distinguish details at a distance.

"Looks like Mrs. Whitworth!"

"Headed this way? Why, it can't be."

For a brief moment, the buggy dropped from sight to traverse a low water crossing. When it came into view, it would be headed straight at us. It was Mrs. Whitworth without a doubt. She pulled right up to us. She wore a duster to keep some of the dirt off of her. Her hands were gloved, of course. In fact, I can't recall if I had ever seen her hands without gloves. Rachel Whitworth was a very proper churchgoing lady. However, to have lived with the Colonel this long, she had to have some grit to her. She loosened her bonnet and then addressed Grandpa.

"General, you know this has been a difficult ride for me."

"Monaville isn't that far, ma'am."

"Leander, you know perfectly well what I mean. I appreciate that I am not welcome here."

Grandpa said nothing. His face was set, expressionless at best. I could tell that neither he nor Mrs. Whitworth wanted to spend a whole lot of time together.

"Leander, a lot of time has passed. I can see your memory hasn't failed you. Nor can I blame you for your feelings. We do and say things in our younger years that we later regret. You won't believe me, but I've regretted my actions."

Grandpa continued to stare directly at Mrs. Whitworth and made no reply.

"The district attorney has formed a grand jury, and he intends to indict Reams for murder. They are to meet tomorrow evening. As you might expect, the jurors are men very favorable to McCoy and Harrington. Colonel Whitworth tries to make light of it, but these are different times. If Harrington gets the indictment, the right jury could hang Reams. He considers you his best friend. You must do something."

"This is the reason for your trip to Catalpa?"

"Why, yes."

"Then you have misjudged me again, ma'am. I would no more let something happen to Colonel Whitworth than I would let someone harm my grandson. I have already considered my course of action."

"What do you intend to do, General?"

"As I said, I have already considered my course of action. You will see."

The repetition may not have been what Rachel Whitworth wanted to hear. However, she knew better than to ask again.

"I knew you would help."

"No, you didn't, and that is why you made this trip. Good day to you."

The General turned his horse and moved toward the next pasture. I did not know the conversation was over and, apparently, neither did Mrs. Whitworth. We sat there looking at each other, and then it occurred to me that I needed to catch up with my grandpa.

"Good day, Mrs. Whitworth."

"Good-bye, John Ross."

After dinner, Grandpa decided that he, my father, and I ought to make a trip out to the old Baptist church. If the grand jury was going to meet the next evening, he figured that some of the Klan and Ocy McCoy's acquaintances might be getting together.

He placed me in the lead. I took them down a path that I had recently made that was not one of the usual trails to the church. It went through some rather dense underbrush, but actually placed us closer to the church than any of the other trails that I had found, or made. The trail was barely identifiable. I had to hold back some pine limbs for us to gain access to it, and once on the path, we brushed scrub brush on both sides with our shoulders. It was like being in one giant green-briar tunnel.

"Jesus, son, maybe you should have let the hogs work on this route a little more."

"It's tight, Pa, but it leads to a great spot to view the comings and goings of folks." Grandpa smiled. I sensed he kind of liked the scouting trip.

We arrived just as the sun was going down. We dismounted, ground tied the horses, and positioned ourselves along a wooded ravine. In almost no time, riders began to appear, followed by the sheriff and the district attorney. Grandpa suspected that, in large part, this would be a dress rehearsal for the grand jury. Rather than enter the church, they all took seats on the steps of the entrance. T. Roliff Harrington III remained standing.

Between coughs, spitting, and the night noises, it was difficult to hear everything that he said. The Colonel's name came up frequently and always provoked a curse or two from the assembled Klansmen. Some were very interested in expediting the legal process as much as they could in hopes of somehow getting their cotton ginned locally. Harrington anticipated that the Colonel would retain counsel from one of the larger communities. No doubt, there would be delays, unless the people took things into their own hands. Harrington's suggestion certainly fell on fertile ground.

The crowd gradually dispersed, leaving the McCoys seated on the steps of the old church sharing a flask of whatever rotgut liquor they had managed to get their hands on. It took them very little time to finish off their drinking and then they left as well.

"I had Blue mark the shoes of their horses." The General pointed in the direction of the church. "I wanted to make certain that I knew who was riding with this group. We didn't miss anyone."

"What will they do next, Grandpa?" Not being versed in the intricacies of the judicial system, talk of lawyers and grand juries did nothing but confuse me.

"No doubt they will convene a grand jury to indict the Colonel. I suspect we have just seen the members of that group, or at least most of them. However, Colonel Whitworth will never see a trial."

"He won't?"

"No. Didn't you hear what Harrington said? He just planted the seeds of a lynching in the weak minds of those bastards. Given their need to have their cotton ginned and their newfound arrogance acquired from walking in the shadow of the great Mr. Harrington . . . well, it won't be too long before they make their move."

I felt a chill. I wanted to think it was the night air, but I knew it wasn't. Things were getting real serious, real fast.

"John Ross, please lead us out of this labyrinth that you and the hog population of the Brazos Valley have created. Just maybe Momma Mae has a little something left for us."

The next morning and all the next day, Grandpa was preoccupied. There was very little conversation. We went about our daily routine by rote.

*   *   *

Before dinner, the General rode out toward Monaville, only this time he actually intended to go to town. He arrived about dusk and as he entered Main Street, he glanced one block over toward Blue's barn. Thereafter, his eyes were fixed on the courthouse located in the middle of town and, quite literally, in the middle of the road three to four blocks away. His hat was firmly seated on his head, pulled down lower in the front so that the brim blocked more of the setting sun. He had changed out of his work shirt into a heavily starched white shirt. Momma Mae could make them just as stiff as a board. His gray coat still held its color. Neither warfare nor ranching had really faded it all that much. The collar was still upright, but no longer held his stars. However, a closer inspection revealed the stitching that once affixed them to the fabric there. Only one thing about his attire was out of the ordinary—he was wearing his gun belt, which holstered the Colt revolver that he had carried for four very long years.

The establishments on the first block were closed. No one was about. It had been a long time since the General had been in Monaville proper. The War had not visited here. However, the financial impact of it was clearly visible. Most of the buildings were now totally gray. Any pigment that had once been applied to their facades had peeled or worn away. More shutters were hanging loose or missing than were operable. None of this mattered to the General's great bay warhorse. While the bay was older now, his conformation was still good. You'd have thought he was leading a parade down Main Street. He arched his neck slightly, tucking his head down just enough to show onlookers that there was still something regal, something special about him and the rider he carried.

Past the second block, there was more activity. This was where most of the larger commercial interests were located, including the Colonel's store and Nuncio's, but the General stayed focused on the courthouse.

Nuncio's was loud, but not loud enough to muffle the exclamation of one of its more sober customers. "Good God Almighty! Is that General Wilhite?"

"If it is, hell has surely frozen over," came a snappy retort from one of the locals.

Twelve or thirteen noses were immediately pressed against the glass window of Monaville's finest drinking establishment. The General traveled past them, maintaining a slow, even pace.

Rachel Whitworth's house was by far the largest one on the next block. In the evenings, she and the Colonel enjoyed the quiet of their veranda. She would sip coffee and he would sip something a good deal stronger out of his coffee cup. After all, they were within sight of the new Baptist church.

Rachel's cup dropped, crashing against its saucer, causing the Colonel to glance up from his paper at his wife. "Oh my God, Reams . . . is . . ." The Colonel followed her gaze.

"Well, darling, this could get real interesting real fast."

Neither moved. The General continued down Main Street, now leaving quite a number of gawkers staring after him, perplexed and a little uncomfortable.

The courthouse was once a rather impressive building—a three-story brick structure. The bricks were handmade by slaves who dug the soft red clay from the banks of the river. Even though they were handmade, the bricks showed more uniformity than you would expect. Every so often, you would find one that showed where the heel of someone's hand had hit the clay a little harder than necessary. Maybe those indentions quietly expressed someone's weariness with brick making or perhaps his general frustration with his lot in life. Like every other building across the south, the courthouse was in desperate need of paint.

The General hitched the bay next to the other horses standing along the east side of the courthouse. As he passed behind each horse, he studied their tracks, noting the markings Blue had placed on their horseshoes.

Judging by the horses, he hadn't missed anyone when he'd made his list, and they were all here now.

The building was closed and dark, except for a dim light coming from the basement. The Texas heat made the basement the favorite room for jury deliberations, which could sometimes get heated. The cooler basement was welcomed. The door was slightly ajar. The General pulled it open, causing its hinges to scream for some lubrication. Wooden steps led directly to the jury room. From the door, the General could only see the basement floor, and the jurors could not see who had opened the door.

The General's first step caused the wooden stair to creak, but when the bois d'arc wood of his right leg hit the second step, all conversation in the basement ceased. Another creaking sound was followed by the sound of his bois d'arc peg striking the oak step. The pattern of sounds continued for what seemed like an eternity to those assembled in the basement. Sweat beads formed on the foreheads of those men who had ridden their marked horses to Monaville to reach the foregone decision to indict Colonel Whitworth for the murder of Ocy McCoy. Complexions ruddy from the Texas sun now looked pasty and pallid. At the last step, General Leander Wilhite stood directly at the end of the table facing the district attorney who was seated at the other end. Mr. Harrington's minions were seated as well, but were clearly uncomfortable in the presence of the General.

General Wilhite glanced at a figure in the far corner of the room. For reasons that could only be explained by examining the alcohol-filled brain of Monaville's sheriff, M. E. Brown suddenly jumped to his feet and just as quickly sat back down.

Harrington spoke first with a slight tremor in his voice.

"General, this is certainly a surprise. You don't frequent Monaville very often."

"Sir, it is no greater surprise than a Texas grand jury indicting someone for murder when it was patently obvious that it was self-defense."

"You do get directly to the point, General. However, this grand jury will do what the law requires it to do."

"This so-called grand jury will do whatever you want it to do. Do understand that its decision will be your decision, sir. If that decision is to indict Colonel Whitworth for murder, there will be trouble. Trouble the likes of which you men have never seen."

The General's gaze circled the table, boring deeply into the eyes of each man seated there. He turned and ascended the stairs.

He retraced his route down Main Street, and although he appeared to trot out of town, he actually circled back to Blue's barn. He dismounted at the rear of the barn and walked his horse to an interior stall. Blue came out of his quarters.

"My, my, dis is a surprise. Howdy dere, General."

"How are you, Blue?"

Blue glanced around and saw the bay horse standing in a stall.

"General, you and me, we gotten older, but dat bay looks as good as he eber did."

"Blue, would you mind easing down the backstreet and bringing Colonel Whitworth here?"

"Would I . . . no, sir, do it right now." Blue disappeared out the back door headed in the direction of the Colonel's home. In no time at all, they returned to the barn.

"General, I didn't hear any shooting; I must say I was disappointed that you didn't kill them all."

"Very sound strategy, Colonel. Then both of us would be indicted for murder."

Blue smiled quietly and took a seat on a nail keg.

"Colonel, every man in that room is a coward, and a desperate one at that. Some for different reasons, but still desperate nonetheless. We must act quickly or you will be a dead man."

"Aw hell, Leander, my lawyer will tie this thing up in knots. It will be a coon's age before trial."

"There won't be a trial. You will never see a courtroom. I will work out the details. Luther will visit with you about them in the next day or so. What he tells you to do, you do."

"Leander, you know I will, but do you really think a carpetbagger and some drunken croppers have the gumption to start something?"

"Reams, stay in town and in public view."

The General retrieved the bay from its stall. He left Blue's barn at a clipped trot, and by the edge of town, he and the bay were in an easy canter back to Catalpa.

CHAPTER 12

Rack Is Back

THE NEXT MORNING, THE General delayed our departure until my father came to the barn. He was always somewhat slower, being the only married man in the house. As he saddled his horse, Grandpa gave us both a summary of the previous night's events. My pa and grandpa no longer went outside the barn to discuss matters. I could only guess that my scouting efforts had earned me the right to listen. Grandpa explained his plan and then told my father to head to Monaville after lunch. My pa was to take a wagon and pick up supplies at the Colonel's store, while we went off on our usual rounds of the plantation. Although the General wanted to move fast, he did not want to call any attention to his plan.

Throughout the next day or so, my pa quietly left Catalpa to visit six or seven men selected by Grandpa from his old army company. After each visit, my pa advised Grandpa that he had the support of each of his old comrades—he just needed to give the order. They all understood the mission. Every report from my pa created a higher level of nervousness in me. All these men had seen combat, while I still thought of myself as Miss Hightower's pupil.

I took some comfort in the fact that so many men were willing to follow the General wherever he might lead them. Their support for the Colonel was just as strong. As we went about our chores, I did what I could to organize all the facts and issues of the situation. However, I got hopelessly lost when I pondered the legal system. Timing seemed to be especially critical. T. Roliff Harrington III, as the district attorney, was in control of the legal proceedings. Following the election, he would likely be county judge, a position even more powerful than the one he currently held. Needless to say, none of these issues ever came up back when I was in Edwina Hightower's classroom.

Arriving back at the barn after checking the cows, I unsaddled the horses—Grandpa's and mine. I felt mentally exhausted. Too much time spent on issues far beyond me had left me fatigued and numb. A slight breeze was blowing toward the barn, filling it with the smell of damp leather, sweaty horses, and equally sweaty men. Then, it carried in an aroma that was overwhelming in its strength, but vaguely familiar. I turned in the direction of the opened barn door half expecting to see a carcass of some animal lying at the entrance. Instead, standing before me was what was left of Dale. He was far more emaciated than I remembered. His chest was terribly sunken, his clothes mere rags.

My sudden expression of shock caught my grandpa's attention. He looked first at me and then turned in the direction of the door.

"General."

"Dale, I can hardly believe it's you. Are you well? Son, you look terrible."

"Sir, I'm sorry to trouble you . . ."

"Dale, you aren't troubling me at all. Come sit down. You look exhausted."

"I am a little weak, sir, but I wanted to get here as soon as I could."

"Is there a problem, Dale?"

"Sir, Rack is back." The mention of the name caused my pa to glance in the direction of the General. Neither changed their composure, but both were very quiet.

The General moved over next to Dale, pulling a barrel near him.

"Are you sure, Dale?"

"No question, sir. I first saw his tracks two days ago. I hid in the thicket, where I caught a glimpse of him. Then I waited until I felt it was safe to leave the river bottom. I'm real sorry to bother you, sir, but I felt you'd best know."

"Of course, Dale, I appreciate your concern and you're no bother. You don't look well at all."

"I've had some chills and fevers . . . I guess they'll pass."

"I think it's best you stay here with us for a while. It certainly isn't safe for you to return to the bottoms, and I'm not sure your health would stand it much longer, anyway. But we're going to have to get you cleaned up before you come into the house."

"Oh, sir, I can't come into your house, not now . . . not ever. Just wouldn't feel right, no, sir."

"Luther, let's get some water drawn and maybe you could find some clothes that John Ross has outgrown. Dale doesn't look very big. I suspect John Ross is closest to his size."

I went back to my chores, not really knowing if this was a private conversation or not. Grandpa was clearly concerned about Dale and his condition. It almost hurt to look at him. He was just barely alive. It must have taken all he had to walk out of the bottom and make it to Catalpa.

Dale was clearly uncomfortable now, being among people for the first time in years. It was pretty obvious that the hermit of the Brazos needed some help. Grandpa sensed all this. His years as Dale's guardian during the War provided him with some idea of what Dale might find acceptable. Grandpa decided that Dale would bunk in the tack room. Actually, we had all bunked in the tack room at some point. We used it when we needed to sit up with a mare or sick animal. It was warm, certainly better than the cold ground that Dale had been using as a bed.

After dinner, I carried some of Momma Mae's best fixin's to him. He was sound asleep. Normally, I wouldn't have roused him, but he needed food more than he needed sleep. I suspected that Grandpa would permit him to stay here until he got his health back.

He was a good bit cleaner now, and wore clothes that I had worn six or seven years ago. There just wasn't much left of him, and even these garments hung loose on his skeletal frame. After a few tugs and a shake or two, he seemed to come back to life.

"Oh, John Ross, I must have dozed off."

"I'll say. Dale, here's a little something that Momma Mae put together for you. I suggest that you eat it all. You're pretty much down to skin and bone."

"I doubt that will be a problem. I recall the taste of her food. Thoughts of her food snuck into my mind plenty down in the river bottom."

"As good as her food is, her potions are downright terrible. We need to get some meat on you before she sees you, or you'll be findin' out how gawd-awful terrible they are. She has quite a few, and I don't know which one she might pick, but it will sure set you back."

Dale smiled and started his meal in earnest. As I turned to leave, Grandpa entered the tack room.

"How's our patient? He looks a good bit cleaner."

"Thank you, sir."

"Let me visit with Dale a minute, John Ross. After all the solitude in the river bottom, too many folks may make him uncomfortable."

"Sure, Grandpa, I was just leaving."

*   *   *

The General cleared some rope and tack from a bench and sat down, saying nothing for a minute. This gave Dale time to get into his meal.

"Dale, why the river bottom?"

"Sir?"

"You didn't return with the rest of us. Why hide in the bottom?"

"I was ashamed, sir."

"Ashamed of what?"

"I had failed you and you lost your leg because of that."

"Oh, I seriously doubt that, Dale. You're not the one who fired that minnie ball at me."

"If I had moved out quicker when you told me to go for the reserves, relief would've been there, and you wouldn't have had to expose yourself so."

"Dale, we were all just marking time. Every engagement brought each of us closer to a bullet and closer to the end of the War. It was anybody's guess which would come first."

"But I hesitated . . ."

"You went to the War an orphan, no parents, damn little education, and even less in the way of direction. You participated honorably in the worst conflict that could ever visit a country, this one or any other. Blood fought blood. You just never developed any confidence in your abilities. You were always better than you thought you were. If you hesitated, it was due to your own self-doubt. Frankly, I feel damn lucky to have had you with us and even luckier that I made it through with nothing more than the inconvenience of a wooden leg."

Dale's eyes filled with tears. He could not speak. The General continued, "You aren't going back to that bottom. I want you to remain here until you're healthy . . . in the tack room if you prefer, but you are welcome in the house anytime. There are candles here, and I'll fix up an oil lamp in the morning. Behind that saddle is a loaded pistol. We've always kept it in here in case of snakes or varmints. You haven't been around Monaville, but things are uneasy right now.

"About Rack, are you certain that it was him?" asked the General.

"I've only heard of him and his description, but the tracks were his, I'm sure."

"If it is him, he will most certainly head this way. Be mindful of the pistol. You should be aware that we have potential problems with a few other people as well. It's all too complicated to go into just now. Let me leave you to your dinner."

"Thank you, sir."

"One more thing, Dale. When we all came home, I closed the book on the War. I saw nothing productive in rehashing it. Oh, my grandson is sorely put out with me because I don't entertain him with tales of grand cavalry charges. But you and I know they weren't that grand given the friends we lost in the process. I have tried to start anew and move forward. That's my advice to you as well."

"Yes, sir, thank you, sir."

"Good night, Dale." The General stepped from the tack room into the barn. Glancing at his bay horse on the way out, it seemed as if his steed had heard and understood everything.

The next day Dale looked a good bit better. His appetite was everything one could desire for a patient who had seemed to be at death's door twenty-four hours earlier. The threat of Momma Mae's potions moved matters along. He begged Grandpa to let him ride along with him. Grandpa was hesitant, but agreed that he could ride until noon, and then he must return to the tack room and his bunk for some much-needed rest.

This was the opening I had been waiting for. My morning route would take me closest to Monaville, which would give me a chance to slip into town. Dale's mention of Rack last night seemed to provoke some concern in both my grandpa and pa. They had each glanced at each other as if to say, "I'm concerned, but let's visit later." Colonel Whitworth was now on my dance card. I intended to see if my inquiries about Rack would provoke a response or a postponement. He had promised to answer my questions if he felt I was old enough.

Given the current state of affairs, I rode to Blue's, left my horse, and then walked up the alley to the warehouse behind the Colonel's store. He was in and out of that warehouse a dozen times a day checking inventory and moving stock from it into the store. I took a seat among the stacks of merchandise and had barely gotten comfortable when his rotund mass came into the building.

"Howdy, Colonel. Could I have a word with you?"

"Master John Ross, odd that you are now inhabiting my warehouse. What can I do for you?"

"Do you remember telling me that if I had any questions, I could come to you and if you felt I should know the answer, you would tell me?"

"Yes, and no doubt you have such a query?"

"Query?"

"Question, Master John Ross, question. What is it?"

"Last night, Dale—you know Dale?"

"Yes, of course, the hermit of the Brazos."

"Yes, sir. He came to our barn."

"Did he? That alone is news."

"Yes, sir, he told my pa and grandpa that he had seen Rack in the river bottom. They seemed to be very concerned. Isn't Rack the slave who killed Blue's sister?"

"Elisabeth. Yes, go on."

"That's pretty much it, sir. Why are they so concerned? Why hasn't the law gotten him years ago?"

"Dale isn't that old. I can hardly believe he could identify Rack," said the Colonel.

"He said he saw his tracks and caught a glimpse of him."

"Ah, that makes sense. If it is Rack, his timing couldn't be worse. My current unpleasantries with the law seem to have your grandfather a little occupied. To answer your question, your father and grandfather would be concerned. Let's move away from the door a little. I suspect you waited in the warehouse for me so you wouldn't be seen."

"Yes, I thought it best."

"Let me organize my thoughts . . . Oh, hell, I'll tell you the whole damn episode, or most of it. I understand you're Leander's scout now. He must place a good deal of confidence in you. I should do likewise.

"It all started back in slave times. Leander was bitten by the blooded-horse fever, meaning he was running a number of horses on the racetrack. It is a sickness, I tell you. When you get it, you

Why Rack didn't hear Leander coming, I'll never know. All the slaves in that bottomland stopped what they were doing. Some of the women just gasped.

"Rack backed up, post in hand, and moved to the front of that mule. Then, with a huge terrible swing, he arched that post over Ink's head and brought it down so hard that it killed that animal right there in its harness. Leander was in full gallop leaning over his saddle horn as if he was taking flight.

"I expected him to stop short and beat the hell outta Rack. He didn't. Rack still didn't hear your grandfather, but he either sensed the motion or noticed the stillness among the other slaves. He turned in the direction of the General just seconds before the chest of that horse hit him square on. Now I had heard some awful sounds during the War, sounds that would make you want to throw up. But I'll never forget the sound of the concussion between Rack and that horse. It knocked that man out cold.

"Leander turned his horse around, grabbed his lariat, and galloped back. With very little effort, he roped Rack's feet and headed off, again in a full gallop, dragging his limp body behind him. As Leander rode away, I could tell Rack's right arm was broken . . . broken clean. How far he dragged him, I never asked. When he came back, he and his saddlebred horse dragged the mule out of the field."

"Good Lord, I can't believe that didn't kill Rack."

"Would have been far better on several counts if it had."

"I'm surprised he didn't kill 'em."

"John Ross, killin' isn't as easy as you think. I hated Yankees with a passion, but even then it weighed on me when I had to send one to meet his Maker. Who knows—another time, another place—we might've been friends."

"What happened then?"

"I think Leander hoped that Rack would hole up in the bottom, see the light, and come back at some point. It happened all the time. The bottomland was filled with slaves hiding out for various reasons—sometimes it was as a result of too little discipline; sometimes, too much. Occasionally, a slave had just gone out on a lark and was concerned about the discipline that might be coming his way when he returned.

"Rack did return one more time and then left for good. It had been at least a couple of months since he had killed ol' Ink. All the slave folks were out in the field, except for Elisabeth, Blue's sister. She was nursing an infant boy back at the quarters. Somehow Rack found his way there and killed her. We all tried to track him. A three-toed man isn't hard to track, but he knew the bottomland and was never found. My guess is he hung on to the side of one of the riverboats until he got down to the coast. He must have moved fast, or we would have caught him. Momma Mae took the little boy, a skinny light-colored baby. She was wet at the time and nursed him while she nursed her own little boy. That's when she started to hum like she does. I suppose she was trying to give some comfort to the little ones.

"You can see why the General is concerned. Rack has brought nothing but violence to Catalpa. If he has come back—although why he would is beyond me—then he must be stopped."

"I understand."

"Master John Ross, it is time for me to return to my paying customers. I do hope that is your only question for today."

"Yes, sir, I suppose."

The Colonel moved toward the store. I waited for a moment and then headed to Blue's and back to Catalpa. I was exhausted and that was just from listening.

CHAPTER 13

Justice

MY SCOUTING DUTIES CONTINUED, and each evening either my pa or grandpa went with me. We half expected to see some change in the Klansmen's pattern, but the only real change was that several croppers had abandoned the effort since Grandpa's visit to town. The regular attendees were the four McCoy relatives, still smarting over the death of Ocy. They pretty much stayed in Monaville and engaged in big talk at Nuncio's. Apparently, their plans for harvesting their cotton crops were on hold.

The McCoys were in rare form in front of the old church on Friday night. The Colonel's name was mentioned much too frequently for comfort. The General sensed that they would return on Saturday evening, either to finalize their plans, or perhaps, to proceed with them then. Harrington and Sheriff Brown could be expected to join them on Saturday night. The six remaining Klansmen—the McCoys, Harrington, and Brown—rounded out a very manageable group for the General and his comrades.

Saturday morning, the General sent my father to inform the select few that they would be needed that evening. The Colonel was notified as well. After closing his store, he and Blue were to meet at Blue's barn, bringing a wagon and certain items. On his way back to Catalpa, my father sought out Big Charlie, who was told to be at our barn later to ride with us. The General maintained his usual daily routine, and so did I. He also maintained his usual stoic composure, whereas I was a complete bundle of nerves.

Toward the end of the day, he asked me if I was scared. I, of course, wanted to impress him with as much bravado as I could muster. He was not convinced, but put my mind at ease, somewhat.

"John Ross, being scared can be a good thing. Sometimes it will keep you alive. If you want to fear something, then fear complacency because that's what will get you killed. I must tell you that I don't like what we're going to do, and I detest the need to do it. It shouldn't be my chore, but if I don't do it, no one else will. Do you understand that?"

"Yes, sir."

"I don't want you to think bad thoughts about me. There are things in life that you must commit to and then do. You can't agonize over things. Remove the doubt and go. I'm not saying you should be rash or hasty, but once the path is clear, delay becomes your enemy. It is painfully obvious to me that these people have killed before, for no good reason. Now they have all kinds of reasons to want Colonel Whitworth dead. Plus, they are protected by the sheriff and the district attorney."

We were on the road leading home. His words weighed heavily on me; yet, I knew he carried all the real responsibility.

"It is my greatest hope that tonight's events will return Monaville back to the time that I once knew. Maybe it will once again be a place where young people like you will want to spend their days. It has not been easy for your father or me to include you in these matters, but you have a role to play because you are the future. I hope to keep your involvement to a minimum, but you must take part.

"I'm sure you already know this, but what happens tonight must be your life's secret. It must die with you, John Ross."

"Yes, sir, I understand." We were within sight of the barn, and hundreds of thoughts were racing through my mind.

"Don't unsaddle the horses. We'll move out shortly. Get Dale's dinner. As soon as Charles arrives, we'll leave."

My grandpa was the only person in the county who called Big Charlie, Charles. But if he wanted to call him Charles, I was certain it was fine with Big Charlie.

"Is Dale going with us?"

"No, he doesn't have the strength, and he has been away from all of this for so long. I'm not sure he would understand. If he didn't understand, he would have doubts and there isn't time to resolve doubts."

"Yes, sir."

A third-quarter moon was barely visible when we left Catalpa. Evenings were now getting a little cooler. We were going to meet the others at the Wilhite Cemetery. The General had selected six men he trusted from his old company. All had been raised in Monaville. All had left with him shortly after the commencement of the War. Some were slightly older than my father, but none were older than the General. The only common thread among them was their War experience. Short of that, they covered the gamut when it came to occupation, financial position, and appearance. It was clear that their respect for the General was exceeded only by their fondness for the Colonel. They grew quiet as the General approached.

"Men, gather round me if you will." The General was prepared to move out and wanted to go over some last-minute details.

"I know Luther has given you the basic plan. If any of you don't want to be a part of this, you may leave now, no questions asked. I only request that you keep these matters confidential." He paused and looked around at the men and then paused again, looking at his gloved hands resting on his saddle horn.

"Sir, I think we are all ready," said Avery McElroy, nicknamed "the Scotsman." He appeared totally red except for his eyes. He had curly red hair and a ruddy red complexion. All of which drew attention to the bluest eyes you were ever likely to see. He had owned a large plantation before the War, but his family could not hold it together and lost most of it. Now, he just had the house and about 75 acres. His existence was just a shade better than that of a sharecropper—worse in some ways. Each day he could see the ruin-ation of his fields by others who had no heart for farming. Fields that had once been productive were now being rapidly depleted of all their fertility.

"Hell, General, we all knew that sooner or later we were going to have to pull the Colonel's fat out of the fire. I guess we just didn't know there was going to be so much of it."

Everyone enjoyed the joke, which eased some of the tension in the air.

"My grandson, John Ross, will lead us to the old church by some trails that I'm sure you have long forgotten. I expect that there will be six men there—four McCoys, the sheriff, and Harrington. They usually arrive about dark or shortly before. John Ross will position us behind the church and then he will take up a position to watch the road.

"They tend to gather in the front of the church. On my signal, we will move quickly to the front, where I hope to catch them by surprise. If any of them make a break for it, they must not be allowed to get away. Luther, you and the Scotsman will go after any that run. Gentlemen, arm yourselves."

On that command, everyone but me and Big Charlie pulled a Colt revolver, gun belt, and holster from their saddlebags. Somewhere on each holster was stamped the initials "CSA." I'd never seen these men armed, and I must have seen them a thousand times. The simple act of putting on their gun belts seemed to change their demeanor. There was no more kidding. There was business to be taken care of, and their intentions were obvious.

"Colonel, you and Blue drop back a little. You won't be able to take the wagon down these trails. Stay hidden until dark and then come down the back road. John Ross will be looking for you. You should be able to see the front of the church. After we have them, you can join us. John Ross, move out. We'll follow you."

My gulp had to have been audible, I'm sure of it. My grandpa was right behind me, followed by my pa, and then the rest of the men arranged by their former ranks. It was getting dark quickly. I worried that I might not get everyone there in time or that we might be seen or heard. When it was just my grandpa and pa and me, moving through the brambles didn't raise much noise, but how noisy would six more horsemen be? To my surprise, they made no more noise than we had, which probably explained how they survived the War.

By the time we arrived, a soft mist was creeping in from the river bottom. The moisture brought some welcome relief to the dry, brittle hooves of our horses. The General positioned the men in the sloping ravine behind the church. It was not long before the McCoys arrived, already well on their way to a complete drunken stupor. As expected, Sheriff Brown and the district attorney arrived shortly thereafter.

Harrington had dismounted and was in the process of lighting a cigar when the General gave the signal. The men silently divided themselves into two groups, raced past the church, and surrounded the Klansmen with guns drawn. It was so quick that no one said a word. I had expected that the McCoys' response might be somewhat slow, but even the sheriff and Harrington were caught flat-footed. Then the General and Big Charlie appeared, and rode to the center of the semicircle that now enclosed the Kluxers. The sight of the General was shock enough, but the appearance of Big Charlie answered any remaining questions concerning the intent of the General and his men.

"Scotsman, check them for any weapons."

McElroy frisked and disarmed them all, now provoking a response from the district attorney.

"General, what is the meaning of this?"

The General did not answer, but simply looked at the six Klansmen standing before him and, more important, standing before Big Charlie.

"General, just what are your intentions? You at least owe me the courtesy . . ."

"I owe you no courtesy at all, Mr. Harrington. You need no explanation. The presence of this man next to me should explain it all to each of you."

Colonel Whitworth and Blue arrived with the wagon. The General did not even turn to acknowledge them. The War years gave each one of them plenty of insight into what to expect from each other. Colonel Whitworth and Blue started unpacking the crates. While this provided a minor distraction, the tension overcame Sheriff Brown.

"Good God, Leander, you don't plan on killing us, do you? We've been friends forever."

"Brown, I detest each of you. It goes beyond that. You killed a young man who had promise, who had never harmed you, and you killed him for no reason at all."

"'Fore the War, no one would've said nothin'. He was just a . . ."

"Stop, Sheriff. Stop right there. You were a coward before the War, and you are a coward now. Because of you and your failure to stand for any sense of justice, we—the men here with me—are forced to do your job . . . yours and the district attorney's.

"Luther, bind their hands and feet and gag them."

"Leander, please, this isn't right." Brown was shaking visibly.

"No. Brown, it isn't right. If we had honest men in the offices that you and Harrington hold, we wouldn't have to do this."

Luther and the Scotsman positioned the six men against the front wall of the old church. The alcohol was wearing off of some of the McCoys, but just barely.

The General nodded to Colonel Whitworth. He and Blue handed six new carbines to the men who formed the firing squad.

"Men, there is a single bullet in the chamber. Don't miss."

At this point, only the General and Big Charlie remained mounted. Things got strangely quiet. Lightning bugs vanished. Crickets made no sound. The animal world was observing the event in hushed silence.

The General turned to Big Charlie and in a low but direct voice said, "Charles, by everything that is just and right in this world, you should be down there among our men. But you and I both know that if word ever got out that you had anything to do with this, every Kluxer between here and the Sabine would descend on Monaville like a hailstorm. You must let us do this for you."

"Yes, sir, I understand."

"Colonel, please proceed."

Colonel Whitworth took a position to the side of his six comrades—their faces frozen and without emotion. What they would do tonight would avenge a friend, save the life of another, and, perhaps, return peace to their homes.

"Ready."

The six men inhaled, taking their last breath until the deed was complete.

"Aim."

Muscles and tendons contracted, fingers were now in firm contact with the triggers on the new carbines.

"Fire."

A single muscle contraction slammed a firing pin into the back of a bullet, creating a small explosion within the chambers of each carbine, which was just enough to force the stocks into the shoulders of the men holding the rifles, and large enough to launch conical pieces of lead, spinning faster and faster, down the gun barrels. At maximum velocity, the bullets were launched into the cool night air, quickly piercing the foreheads of the targets and coming to rest in the six cranial cavities of the Klansmen. In the process, all possibility of future devilment from these men was ended, and all of the evil that these six men had visited on Big Charlie and others was destroyed.

The corpses fell against the front wall of the church. Colonel Whitworth and Blue gathered the carbines and returned them to the crates.

The General ordered the saddles and bridles removed from the horses of the Klansmen.

"Gentlemen, judging from the poor condition of those animals, I doubt they'll leave the grass in this area for some time." Saddles and tack were left in one pile. The men remounted.

"Gentlemen, please remove your gun belts and place them back in your saddlebags. I would leave them there until you can return them to wherever you keep them without notice. Please divide up. Return to your homes through the fields and pastures. Stay in the underbrush and avoid the roads. Never speak of this evening. Let us all pray that the Almighty God sees the events of this evening as the necessity that we believe it was."

In a burst of emotion, Big Charlie sat limp in his saddle, his calloused black hands covering his tear-soaked eyes.

The General dismissed his men, and each of them left by a different route. I accompanied my father. Grandpa and Big Charlie remained behind.

CHAPTER 14

Revenge

BEFORE OPENING HIS STORE, Colonel Whitworth had returned six, now slightly used, carbines to their cabinet for sale to the unsuspecting public. In time, they would be purchased, their historical significance unknown to their buyers. No one seemed to make much of the absence of Sheriff Brown or T. Roliff Harrington III. Brown could not always be counted on to be bright eyed and sober on any given day. Harrington, well, he was just above the need to keep specific hours or honor any routine. Nuncio's was sufficiently rowdy with or without the McCoys, so they weren't missed. Monaville stayed focused on the business at hand. There was still cotton to be picked and ginned.

The first indication that something might be amiss was a swirling cylinder of turkey buzzards. Some cropper's curiosity got the best of him and he followed the birds to their source. By the time he arrived, all the scavengers in the Brazos River bottom had had their way with the bodies. They were now mingled and intermingled in the front yard of the old church—what was left of them. The only way to really determine who they once were was by identifying the saddles and tack. The horses, as predicted, had not moved from the thick grass growing around the abandoned building.

The widows of the McCoys were informed and then discouraged from visiting the area. This now raised the challenging question of who should investigate the deaths. Sheriff Brown had headed a department of one, namely himself. His part-time deputy, after learning of the event, resigned—now taking a greater interest in farming than he had previously exhibited. Monaville still had a county judge, but his anticipated retirement had provoked or at least raised the political ambitions of the now departed district attorney.

Monaville was abuzz for a couple of days. There was a great deal of speculating. However, no one had seen or heard anything unusual. Reality soon reestablished itself. With the exception of Sheriff Brown, who had earned a lifetime of enemies and few friends, none of the dearly departed were from Monaville. They were transients at best. The collective community felt no great loss. Soon the daily monotony of agriculture distracted the citizens. Without some push, some burning desire for justice, things just fell into the same old routine.

Everyone remotely associated with the cotton crop was now working from can see to can't. This year's harvest looked promising. Bills could be paid. Perhaps a new purchase or two could be managed by a larger family budget. Agricultural vocations just did not permit distractions. It was even questionable if the deaths of these six men could be classified as a distraction. In large measure, the East Texas branch of the Klan managed to keep the life expectancy of a federal agent for the Freedmen's Bureau hovering around six months, and Federals were not likely to concern themselves with the deaths of six Kluxers, here or anywhere else. Sheriff Brown left an empty office and not much else. A dead Yankee lawyer was of no concern to anyone. Crops and farm animals demanded attention and they got it.

My father was spending a good bit of his time at the cotton gin. Catalpa would get credit for some of each of its croppers' production. Therefore, there was a selfish motive to his attention. Most croppers couldn't read or couldn't read well enough to understand the weigh tickets and receipts that now reflected their year of production. The Colonel ran a fair cotton gin. But others seemed to show unusual interest in croppers with a ginned harvest. The thin pieces of paper in blistered and calloused hands were opportunities for the more educated to take the hard-earned efforts of the uneducated. It probably wasn't part of my father's responsibility, but word soon got around that it wouldn't be wise to cheat a Catalpa cropper.

Grandpa and I alternated days between the cattle and the horses, which slightly broke the monotony. It gave the animals a break from us as well. Late in the week, we were finishing up branding the last set of heifers. There were always stragglers and this had cleared out the last group. Grandpa and I were sitting under a shade tree. Actually, he was leaning against it and I was flat on my back in some soft grass. The calves had stopped bawling and were now close to being paired back up with their mommas.

"John Ross, I think it's about time you and I partnered up."

"Partnered up?"

"I heard you say that you want to make Catalpa your home but that you favor the livestock operation over the sharecropper portion. Am I correct?"

"Yes, and by no small amount."

"Then we need to figure out a way for you to make a living here. You know, earn some money and have a stake in what goes on. I figure we could cut out some of this year's heifers for you. We'll have to discuss how many. They could be the start of your own herd. It would give you a chance to have your own operation, and you would be able to sell the calves."

"But how would I pay you back? And I suppose I would need to pay you for room and board also?"

"Oh, I think not, John Ross. Wilhites don't pay Wilhites for living at Catalpa. I don't want to see that practice started. Plus, you're working full time. The heifers that we sort to you will be part of your wages. We'll run the herd together and divide the profit and expenses on a per-head basis. Eventually we'll be full partners, fifty-fifty."

"Grandpa, this is more than I could've ever hoped for."

"Fine. Your pa felt you'd go along with it. We both respect your talents with animals. They're superior to Luther's and mine, so we might as well use them. I believe Luther is the only one of us three who has the patience to deal with the croppers. I suppose we will need to fix you up with some cash."

"Oh, I have a little money, sir. It's in the bank."

"Where did you get any money?"

Now this was rapidly approaching an area that could cause me to fall from grace in my grandpa's eyes.

"You recall that buffalo ropin'?"

"Sure do."

"Broken Feather told me to bet on the buffalo."

"Broken Feather . . . well, I'll be." What started as a small chuckle ended up as an eye-watering, full-bellied laugh.

"So you bet on the buffalo. It goes to show you that good things can happen when two smart men get together—you and Broken

Feather. That does take the cake. You have certainly topped your grandpa. Many years ago, that old buffalo and his partner in crime, Colonel Whitworth, relieved me of a good bit of money. I am thrilled that you recouped some of my losses."

The thought of my grandpa even participating in a buffalo roping surprised and tickled me all at the same time.

*   *   *

Along the river, fall kind of teases us. It starts with a slight, cool breeze one morning and then it goes away for a few weeks—only to return and leave a few more times after that. You can't point to a date and say that fall will begin right then. The earliest fall I can remember started in September, and the latest began in mid-December. Either late or early, fall—and winter—meant a constant struggle for the people and livestock of the Brazos River valley.

Sunday was one of those tantalizing fall mornings. It wasn't a crisp coolness yet—only a few degrees cooler. Cool enough that I could harness the horses to the carriage and not break a sweat. My mother wanted us all to ride together. I could sometimes sense that she was trying to keep her children, one in particular, in some kind of permanent state of childhood, but I no longer considered myself a child. I suspected that my additional duties could've provoked some maternal fear that one of her hatchlings was about to leave the nest. I had grown slightly more tolerant of the twins. While I never would've admitted it, they also seemed to be growing up, albeit in a tangled, intertwined way.

We all managed to get seated in the carriage. My father took the reins from me, and with a quick snap we were on our way to Monaville for several hours of hell and damnation from the pulpit of our church. For no real reason, as we drove past the house, I turned back to look at it. I hadn't noticed it much in the mornings of late.

On the veranda stood my grandpa. He was standing next to one of the columns, but not leaning against it. His old dog was curled at his feet. Grandpa seemed to be resting, almost tranquil as he watched the cattle graze slowly in the adjoining pasture. In his hand, he held a cup. If I had to guess, I'd say it was filled with Momma Mae's darkest coffee. There was something different about him, but it wasn't readily apparent to me. I turned back toward the road. Then, it came to me. I turned around quickly before we got out of sight. Yes, there stood General Leander Wilhite in just his shirtsleeves. The gray coat he'd always worn wasn't to be seen. To be sure, the dress shirt he wore had all the starch Momma Mae could paint on it. Amazing—no gray coat.

*   *   *

The General placed his cup on a table and stepped down from the porch. He made a loop around the house, headed toward the barn. It was the perfect morning for a slow ride across Catalpa. He knew he would enjoy it. His old bay horse would also. Off in the distance, Dale was working, leaning over a berry patch. He had made a good deal of progress under Momma Mae's care, but he seemed so fragile, almost delicate. The War and near starvation in the bottoms had taken a lot out of him. The General was only steps from the barn.

As he opened the door to the barn, a sharp, sudden pain went through his head. Everything went dark. He couldn't get his bearings. The pain in his head caused a throbbing sensation that left him blind and disoriented. He tried to open his eyes but could see nothing but blurred sheets of colored light. He wanted to rub his head, his eyes, but he couldn't raise his arms. To struggle was useless. He resigned himself to sit quietly, hoping that he would regain the use of his limbs. A deep breath brought back some of his vision, but the pain in his head remained. It didn't stop and the General had no way to make it stop. He was as limp as a wet dishrag, but he felt himself being lifted up off the ground.

He took another deep breath. He was in the air and then astride the big bay horse. Time was passing, but he was now becoming more conscious of his surroundings. It was his barn, but it was darker than usual. The barn door was closed; yet he and the horse were headed in that direction. He couldn't see his hands. After a few more blinks and another deep breath he understood that his hands were tied behind him.

By now, although in great pain, his consciousness was rushing back to him. It came in gulps, not small swallows. It was his horse. He was astride it and his hands were tied. The coarseness of the rope around his neck brought him back completely. It ran from his neck, over a timber rafter and then to somewhere he couldn't see. He knew it had to be tied to something.

He looked down at the neck of his horse and followed it up to the horse's ears. That's when he saw him. He was much older, but still recognizable. Attached to his nappy hair were bits of straw and twigs. God only knew how long the bits had been there. He was shirtless. The skin on his chest was dappled white and black. The scarring from the dragging and rope burns was horrific. His right arm had an odd break in it about four inches below the elbow as if it were a second joint. The General's glance moved to the man's right foot. It really wasn't necessary. He knew the toes would be missing. He raised his eyes to meet the hatred and anger that was Rack.

The General said nothing. It made sense. He had been struck on the head just like that mule, Ink, so many years ago. Rack gave a belly laugh and placed the post on his shoulder.

"Da great Massa Wilhite not so mighty now."

Rack's left eye was almost glazed over and totally gray. He now only had about every other front tooth. No doubt his life had been a series of fights and brawls. The General's neck grew crimson and his eyes narrowed to pinholes with memories of their last encounter and the subsequent murder of Elisabeth. Rack had his attention.

"Wha's da matter, cat got your tongue?"

"I generally don't converse with murderers."

"Ha ha ha. Dat's funny. Scared, Massa Wilhite?"

"Rack, you are a sick despicable individual that I should have killed a long time ago."

"You scared, ain't cha?"

"No. Do what you think you have to do."

Dale had noticed the closed barn door, but he didn't think much about it until it nagged at him. He meandered back toward the barn, gathering berries as he walked. From inside the tack room, he could see the rope looped over the rafter. It made no sense. He was confused and his first reaction was to run. Too many years of solitude had left him ill equipped to deal with much of anything. He peered into the barn and a nervous shiver went down his back. He quickly stepped to the interior of the tack room. He wanted nothing to do with Rack. Why was he here? A second glance followed the rope down to the neck of the man who had protected him for four long War years and who now was nursing him back to health. He must do something. He couldn't run for help—that would most certainly cause the General's death. He remembered the pistol behind the saddle.

The General reflected back on that day the rage had built inside him so quickly when he saw Rack inflicting abuse on an innocent animal, one of *his* animals. At the time, he had doubted that he could ever again be so enraged. Then, not all that much later, he was told of Elisabeth's death and his rage had returned.

Rack could see that Leander Wilhite was not going to demean himself. He kicked the ground. His personal quest for revenge would not bring satisfaction today. He might kill the General, but there would be no sport in it. It angered him more than the events of the past.

"You 'member what you dun, yes, I knowed you do. You 'member?"

The General's gaze never wavered.

Rack lifted the post high above his head. As old as he was, he still had the muscle tone of a young man.

"I kill dat mule. Dis time it will be your horse and you."

The tip of the post barely cleared the barn's rafters. It headed downward, propelled by Rack's arm and back muscles and decades of hate. The speed was remarkable. Its impact with the horse made a loud sickening crack, spraying Rack with blood and brain tissue. The horse that had never flinched under fire, that had stood strangely quiet on watch or in battle, buckled and dropped to its knees. In doing so, the eight coils of rope positioned behind the General's left ear slammed into his head, cracking his vertebrae and severing his spinal cord.

The shot was loud and deadly accurate, but late. It caught Rack in his temple, now mixing human and equine blood and tissue. Dale dropped the pistol and ran to the General, trying to support his body to relieve the tension on the rope. Life had left him almost instantaneously. Leander Wilhite was just dead weight.

The door opened suddenly. Momma Mae had heard the shot. The scene was horrifying. She came first to the body of Rack. She knew who he was and the suffering he had brought to Catalpa. The bay was now lying on its side, its eyes glazed in death. Momma Mae could tell the General was gone, but she followed the rope with her hands and untied it. Dale lowered the General until his body rested in the arms and lap of Momma Mae.

CHAPTER 15

Unanswered Questions

IT WAS HARD TO TELL who was more surprised, the preacher or his congregation. After a week of preparation, someone had the audacity to interrupt his sermon, in his church, while he was talking. The preacher was flabbergasted, as was the entire congregation, who'd turned in their seats and now gazed on the hermit of the Brazos.

But Dale no longer looked like a hermit. He was actually clean and shaved, wearing clothes that were presentable. Some people hadn't seen him since he went off to the War as a mere boy. Now, although still weak and somewhat thin, he was fairly pleasant looking. Dale had ridden hard and fast. He was clearly panicked as he searched for my pa. Finally, he called for him.

"Dale, what is it?" asked my father.

"Luther, you have to come. It was Rack."

My father bounded out of the pew.

"I'm taking the horse. Please bring my family home, Dale."

With that he darted for the door and threw himself astride the horse Dale had just ridden to Monaville. I told my mother I was getting a horse from Blue and left her and the twins with Dale. As I ran toward Blue's barn, I recalled everything I had ever heard about Rack. All of it was bad. I couldn't imagine what awaited us at Catalpa.

Entering Blue's barn, I yelled for him as loudly as I could. "Blue, I need a horse, any horse. Rack is back . . . something has happened to my grandpa."

Blue could hardly speak. He pointed to a sorrel. I saddled him as fast as I could and hopped on, not even bothering to adjust the stirrups. I left by the back door with plans to avoid the road and go across the bottomland. It would be the quickest way if the sorrel had any speed at all. Out of the corner of my eye, I saw Colonel Whitworth. His belly was now so large that he seemed to be falling forward; his pigeon-toed feet moved as fast as his short strides would carry him.

By the time I came out of the bottomland, I was about 100 yards behind my pa. His dust was still in the air when I turned down the Catalpa road. When I arrived, he was kneeling by Momma Mae, who was holding my grandpa, quietly rocking back and forth and humming as she always did. The carnage inside the barn was ghastly. Blood was everywhere and had formed deep, dark pools. My grandpa actually looked at peace, like he was just asleep. The damage to the bay was unsettling. He had been such a magnificent horse; for both of them to go at the same time was probably best.

I only glanced at Rack. He had a sinister appearance even in death. How a person could do so much harm was beyond me.

My father removed the noose. Together, we lifted the General from Momma Mae's lap and carried him into the house upstairs to his room. My father positioned him on the bed and told me to go see about Momma Mae. She hadn't moved. Her chin rested against her chest. She was crying. I closed the doors to the barn. I did not want my mother or the twins looking at the gore that remained.

"Momma Mae, let me help you up. This is no place for you."

She didn't acknowledge me initially, but I knew she'd heard me. I didn't repeat myself, but stood next to her. She finally looked up at me, with bloodshot eyes. She nodded. I helped her up. She was so light, barely the weight of a bird. Together we walked to her porch and her rocker.

"John Ross, it's not right. No, it's not right. Such a good man kilt by just a devil. It's not right."

"No, Momma Mae, it isn't."

The shock of the events, my grandpa's death, and the impact it would have on so many things was beyond my ability to absorb. If my loss was great, I knew hers was greater. She had been part of his life forever. She had to feel lost.

The Colonel and Big Charlie arrived on horseback. I assumed that when the Colonel had told Big Charlie, he had wanted to come along. Blue followed shortly thereafter in a wagon. They all went into the house first to check on my father. By the time they came back out, Dale and my family had arrived.

I told my mother what little I knew and suggested she and the twins avoid the barn. They made their way over to see about Momma Mae. The men gathered around Dale, who had to tell and retell what he knew. I kept thinking about how Grandpa had looked on the porch just a few short hours earlier. How could such tranquility end in such violence?

Before they went into the barn, the Colonel asked Blue if he really wanted to go inside. Blue was adamant. He wanted to make sure the bastard was dead. Tears pooled in his eyes when he looked down on the wretched mass that had been Rack. Old memories came alive again. When he turned to the bay horse, he shivered. I was standing behind him.

"I take care of da bay, John Ross. Don't worry, I take care of da bay."

I wasn't exactly sure what he meant, but I should've guessed. That evening, he and Big Charlie dug the grave for that horse in a corner of the paddock where Grandpa had kept him. When they finished, they left with Rack's body. Whether he got a burial is anybody's guess.

The funeral plans got worked out that evening. I was not privy to any of that, but spent my time with Momma Mae in the kitchen. She started cooking and cooking. I guess she expected a crowd, or preferred cooking to crying. About dark, she gave up cooking for a while and sat down in her rocker with her snuff bottle. I was at a loss for words and didn't know what subjects to mention or avoid. She broke the silence—she and her creaky rocker.

"John Ross, it's nice of you, but ya don't have to stay here wif me."

"Oh, I know, I just don't know if I'm ready for bed." That was actually a lie. The stress and emotion of the day had left me exhausted.

"Lots of men never knows a man like your grandpa. You lucky. You knowed him and he was your grandpa. Spent time, and a lot of it, wif 'em. A man like dat leaves a big hole in everybody. You gonna be lost, John Ross. When you get dat way, you think what he would haf done. You be fine. Now you go get some sleep and leave dis old woman wif her memories."

"Yes, ma'am." I headed for bed. The evening's quietness could not hide her sobs.

The coffin was made from pecan trees that grew in the river bottom. We call them pig or horse pecans because the nut doesn't get very big. I had seen a lot of that wood burnt for cooking but had never seen anything made out of it. It was naturally distressed, with black lines flowing through the grain every so often. They dressed him in his uniform. They'd replaced the stars on his collar where they still caught enough light to draw your attention to them. A red dress sash crossed his waist. His hands held his riding gloves. You knew you were in the presence of a General.

He was placed in the front parlor. A member of his company stood next to him at all times. Early Tuesday morning, twelve old women from Big Charlie's sugarcane operation came to pay their respects. With them they brought more wildflowers than I knew existed in the entire Brazos River bottom. They arranged them and then left as quietly as they had come.

Gustav Weiberg and his wife were next. They still seemed humbled by Grandpa's willingness to share the Wilhite Cemetery.

Colonel Whitworth arrived early and stayed the entire day. His wife did not come; nor did any of the other wives or so-called church ladies of Monaville. There was a constant stream of men, most of whom had been with him in the War. Late in the afternoon, Afton and her father came by. They offered some explanation as to why her mother didn't attend. While Grandpa's friends were there, the grieving process did not seem so personal. When Afton came, I realized how personal it was. I had no ability to detach myself when my friend was there to share the grief.

Toward evening, the men loaded the coffin in Blue's wagon. I remember Colonel Whitworth giving a eulogy, but for the life of me, I can't recall a word he said.

I slept too long the next day. It embarrassed me and made me feel a little ashamed for not getting up on time. No one said anything about it. But it just wasn't right. I forced myself into the daily routine that my grandpa and I had followed. That predictability was now somewhat comforting. I knew where he wanted me and when. Still, it was so unnatural without him.

Sometimes, at the end of the day, I would be unsaddling my horse and I would start to say something to him. Nothing important really. Maybe just an idea about the cattle. The words would be half out of my mouth as I turned toward the bay's stall. No Grandpa. No bay.

About a week after my grandpa's death, Dale left. He didn't say anything to anyone. I know he didn't return to the bottom. I suppose he had his own reasons. Some felt Dale's hesitancy had just resurfaced. If his shot had been a few seconds earlier, Grandpa would still be here. Regardless, there really was nothing to hold him here or in Monaville. He was pretty much alone before the War. He was certainly alone in the bottom. Now that Grandpa was gone, he had no family and was alone again.

Momma Mae quit humming. I didn't want to ask her why. It had always seemed so peaceful. I prayed she would start again, but she didn't.

My father came to depend on me more and more. Like Grandpa expected, he handled the croppers. I stayed focused on Catalpa's cattle and horses.

The Monaville cotton crop had been picked, ginned, and pressed. Most of it left by way of the river. It had been a decent crop even for the worst farmers. But in that line of work, each year stands on its own. Colonel Whitworth was pleased that some of the red ink in his account books had been reduced.

It was now clearly fall. The seasonal struggle between cold fronts and heat waves had stopped. Northerly breezes rattled the big leaves of the cottonwoods around Blue's barn until they fell, only to be crunched under the horse's hooves and the boots of the men of Monaville.

I hadn't returned to Grandpa's grave since his burial. I thought it would take some time for Blue to make the headstone. Of course, I expected him to build his customary fence to make sure all of us Wilhites remained where we were placed. The day was damp. The sky was a monotonous gray sheet without color. I had the time, so I headed toward the Wilhite Cemetery. It sat on the slope of a hill, not at the summit like you might expect. The road went over the top of the hill and that was how it was accessed. I always thought this was a peculiar place for a cemetery until Grandpa's funeral. Then, it all made perfect sense. Horses pulled the carriages and wagons up the hill. Men had to carry the coffin to the grave site. It's a good bit easier to carry a loaded coffin down the slope of a hill than up it.

The cemetery was Blue's pride. Why he took such an interest, I did not know. The iron fence around it seemed to encircle the most impressive oak trees in the valley. There were two front gates, each affixed with a Texas star. The hinges creaked when I opened the gates, but then again, weren't they supposed to?

Grandpa's grave, at the very back of the cemetery, lined up perfectly with the center of the front gates. As I walked in that direction, I passed Wilhite after Wilhite.

The hill fell away from me as I walked down the slope. Grandpa's grave was situated under the canopy of a Texas live oak. Some live oaks had branches that seemed to reach skyward, but the branches of this one grew downward, shading the grave and any visitors, creating a mournful effect.

Around Grandpa's grave, Blue's fencing seemed a little more grandiose than usual. Stars were repeated between the iron uprights. And the entire enclosure was a good bit larger. I opened the gate and stepped inside. The earthen mound had not settled much at all yet. It was hard to believe that under it lay the remains of a man so central to my life. The headstone was perfect. Slightly pointed at the top, the etching was simple and bold—"Leander Wilhite, Major General CSA." I guess that was all that was needed. The position of the grave said it all.

Something seemed odd. I turned back around toward the front of the cemetery. Grandpa's headstone was perfectly aligned with the front gates. However, it was positioned to one side of the fenced enclosure. I glanced toward the flat open area next to his grave and a small, flat stone caught my eye. There was no mound. There had been no recent burial. I knelt down by what I thought was just a piece of limestone, yet it was not weathered. My finger traced the etched letters.

Elisabeth.

Slave. Wife. Mother.